KING OTTOKAR'S SCEPTRE

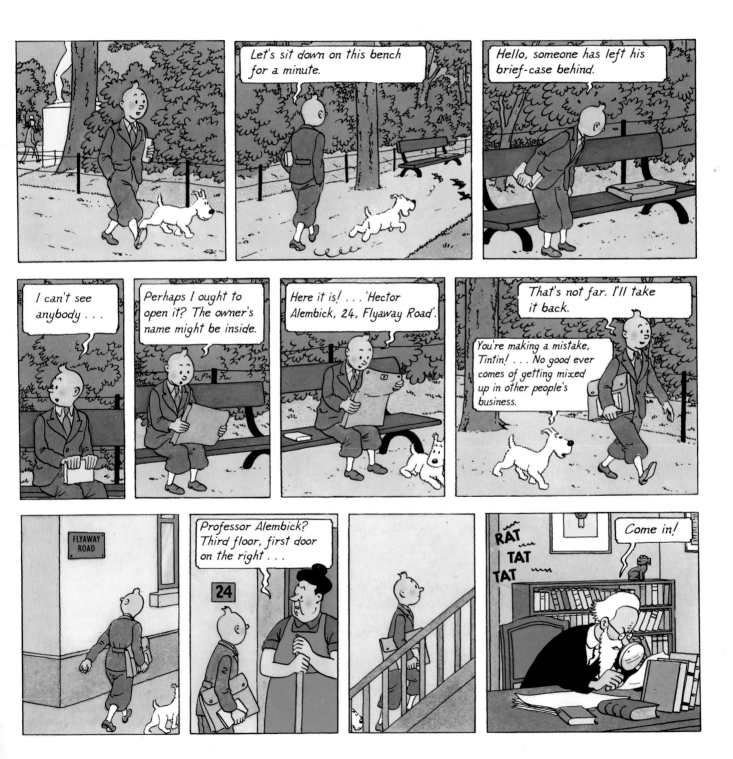

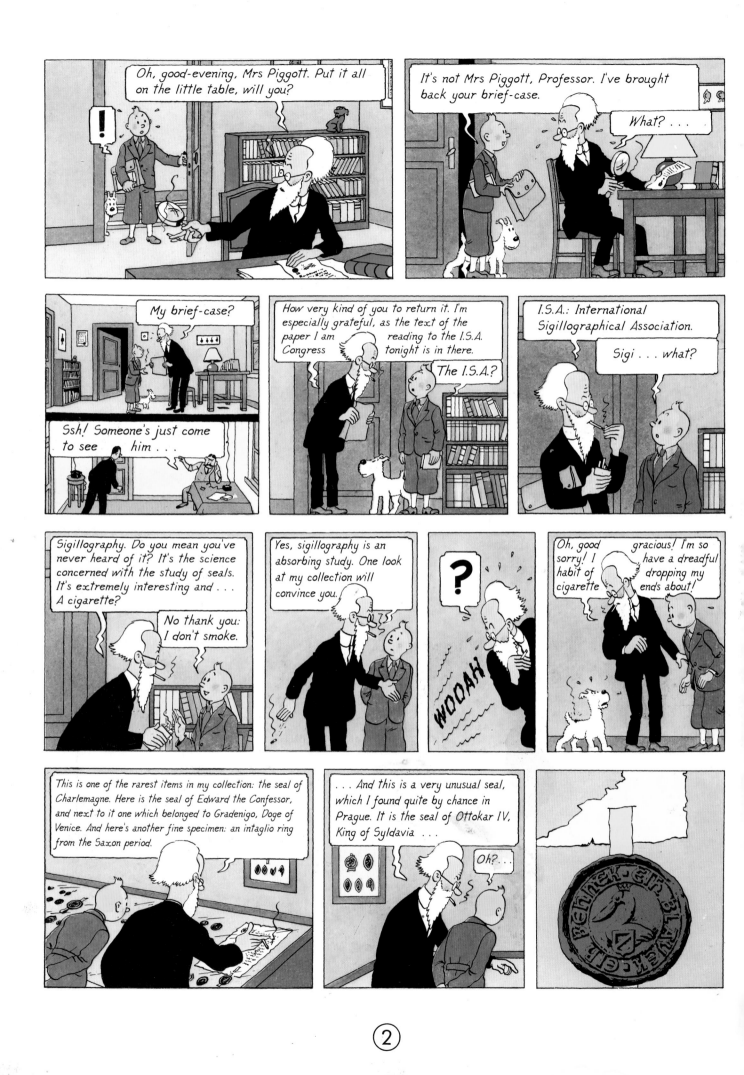

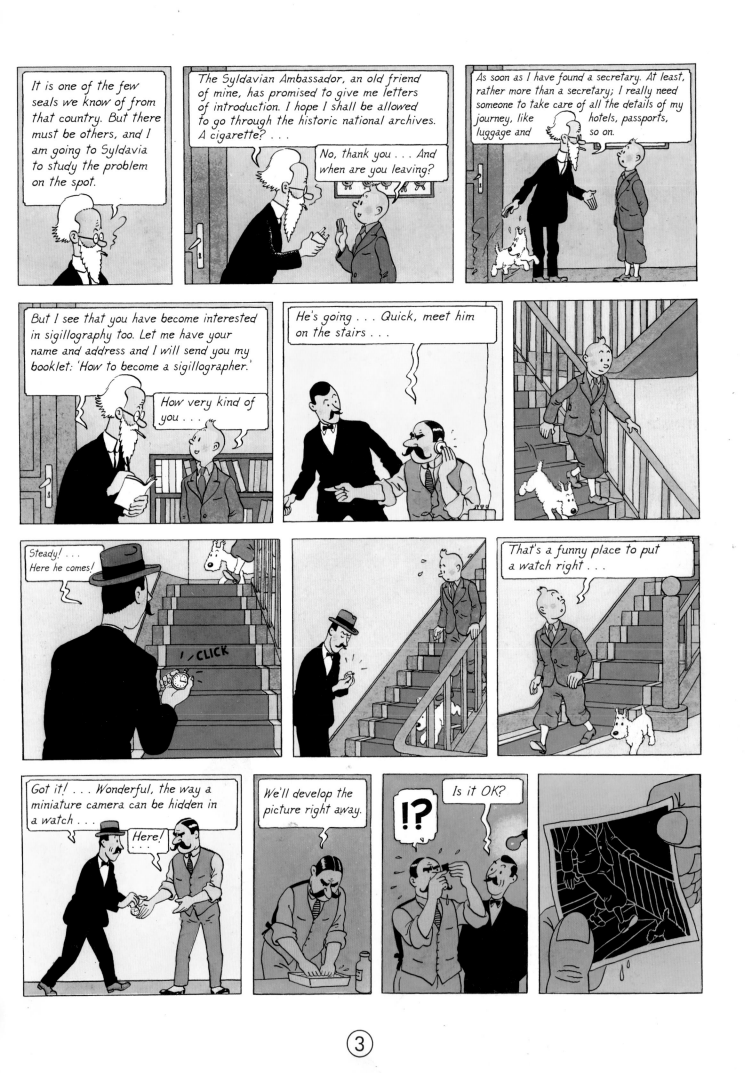

It is one of the few seals we know of from that country. But there must be others, and I am going to Syldavia to study the problem on the spot.

The Syldavian Ambassador, an old friend of mine, has promised to give me letters of introduction. I hope I shall be allowed to go through the historic national archives. A cigarette? . . .

No, thank you . . . And when are you leaving?

As soon as I have found a secretary. At least, rather more than a secretary; I really need someone to take care of all the details of my journey, like hotels, passports, luggage and so on.

But I see that you have become interested in sigillography too. Let me have your name and address and I will send you my booklet: 'How to become a sigillographer.'

How very kind of you . . .

He's going . . . Quick, meet him on the stairs . . .

Steady! . . . Here he comes!

CLICK

That's a funny place to put a watch right . . .

Got it! . . . Wonderful, the way a miniature camera can be hidden in a watch . . .

Here! . . .

We'll develop the picture right away.

!?

Is it OK?

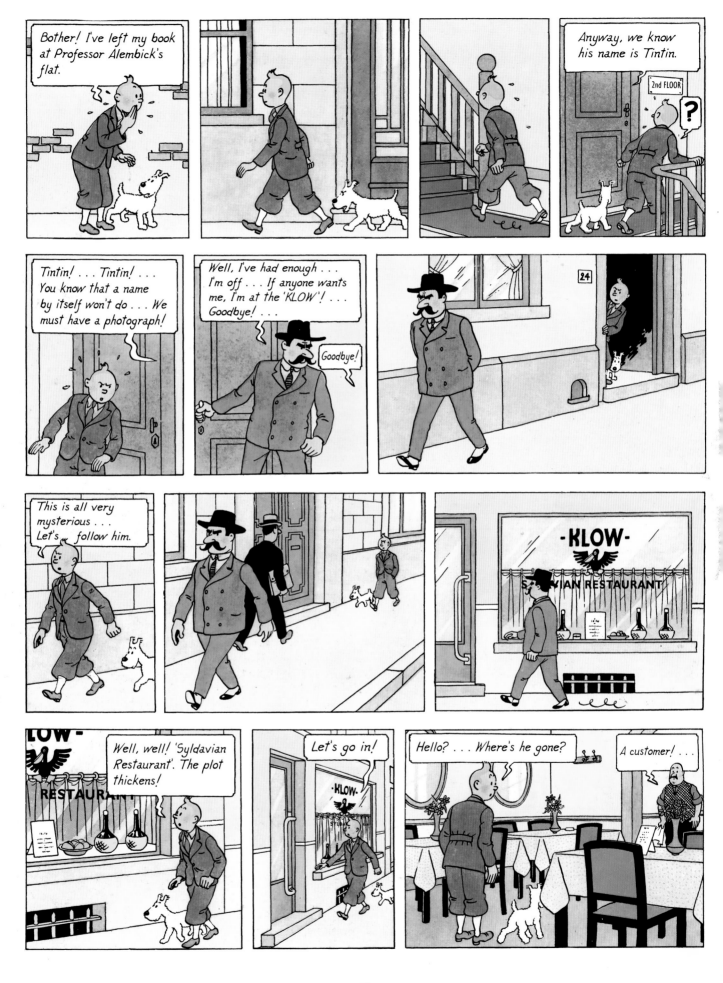

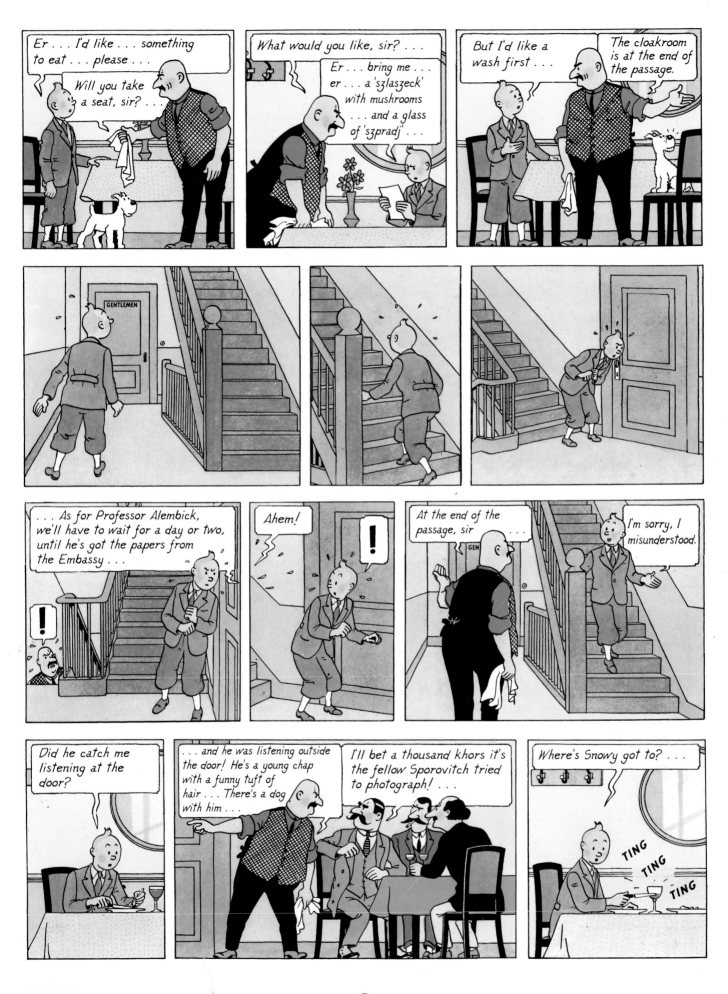

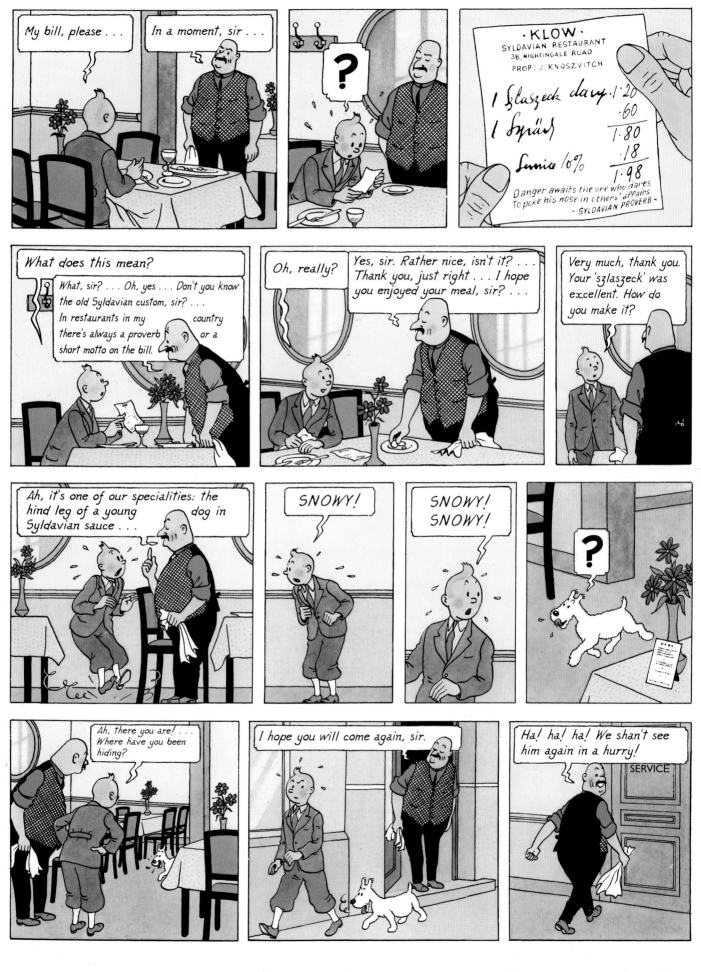

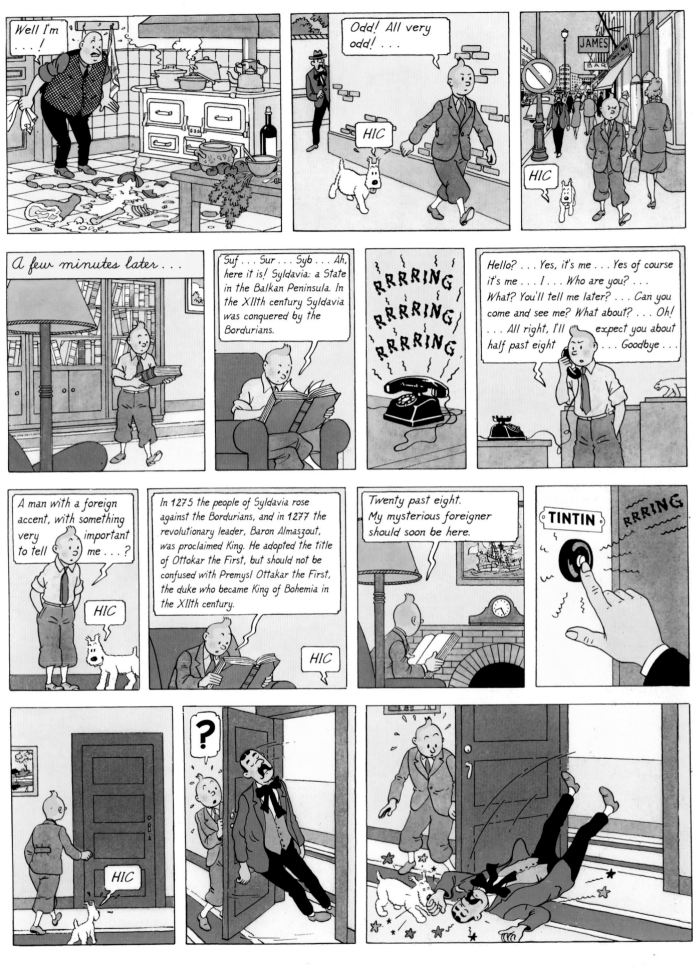

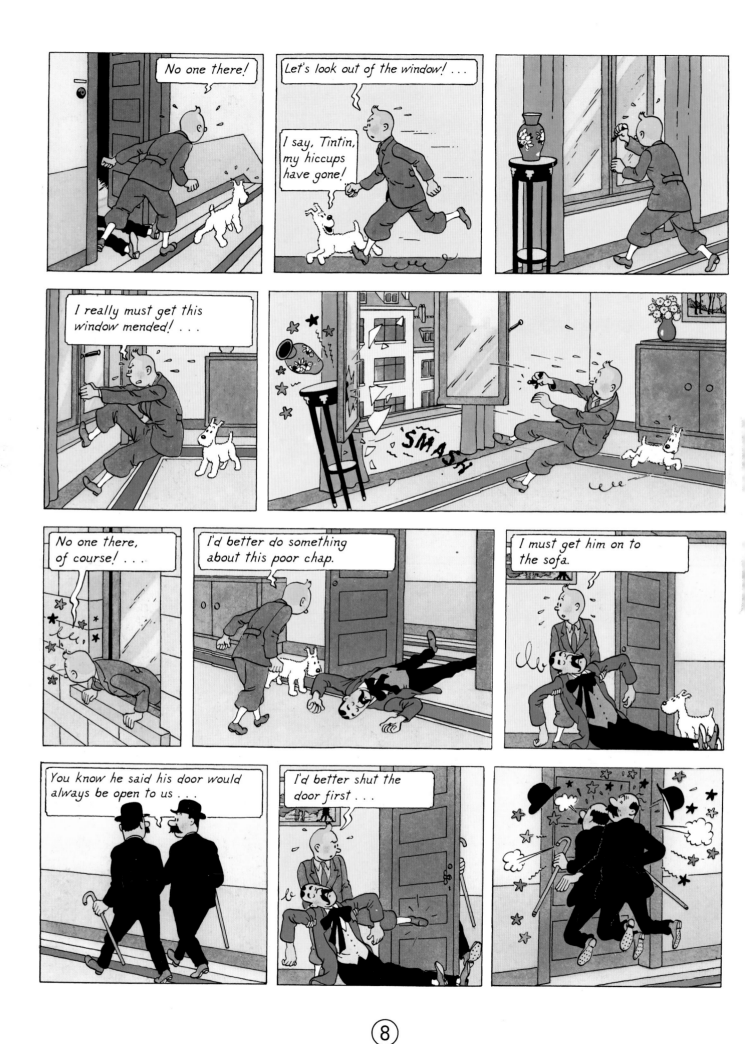

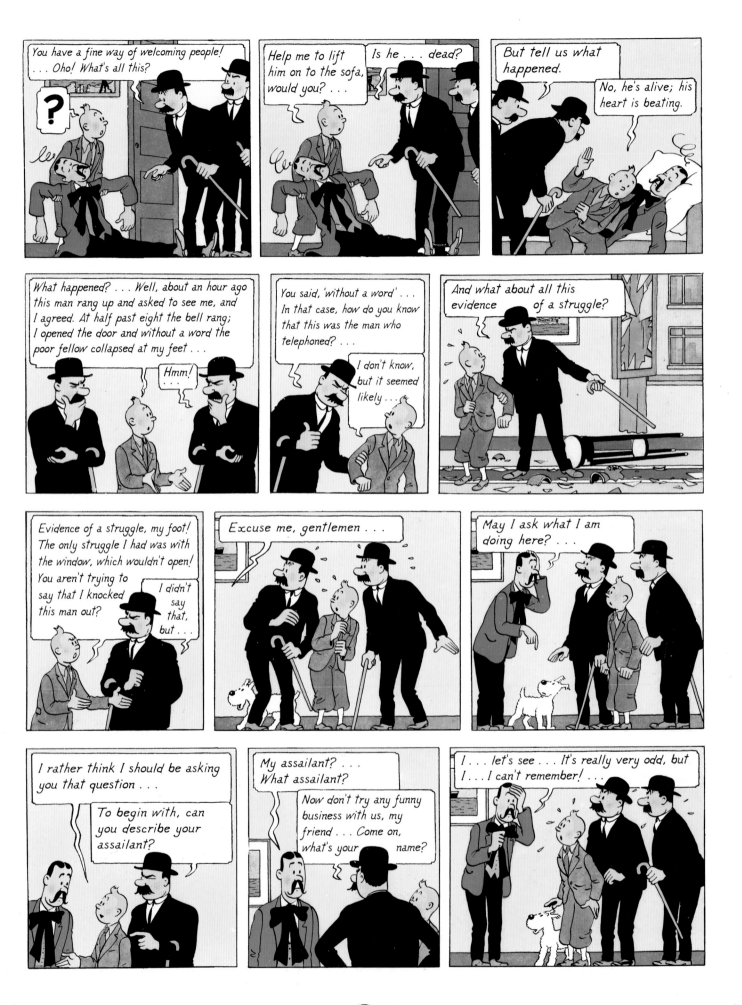

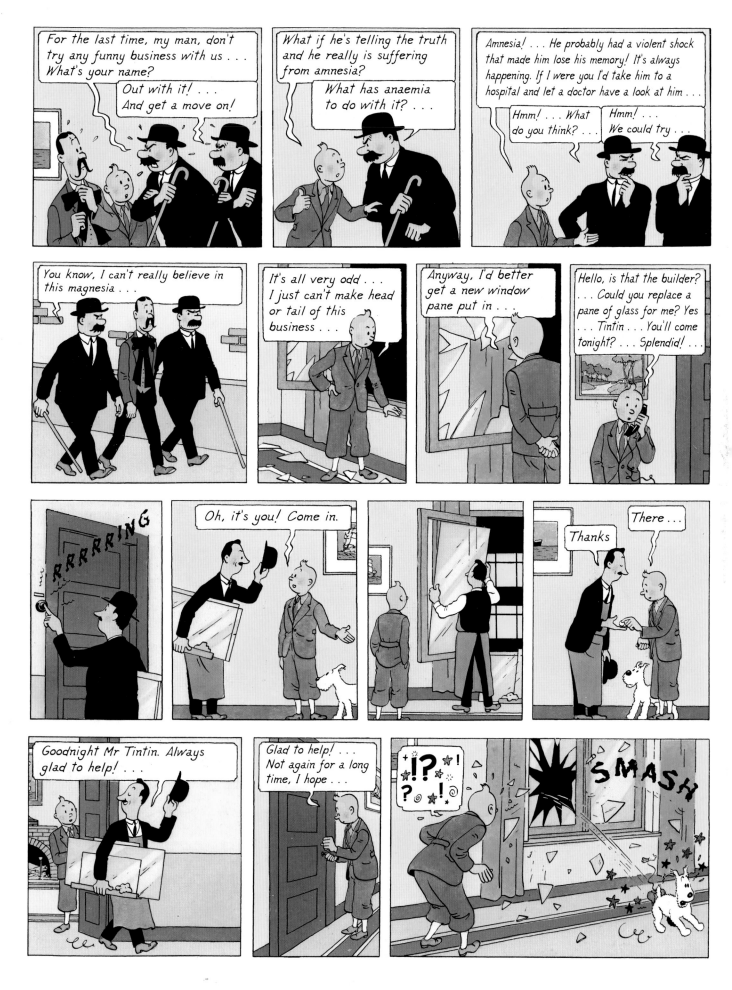

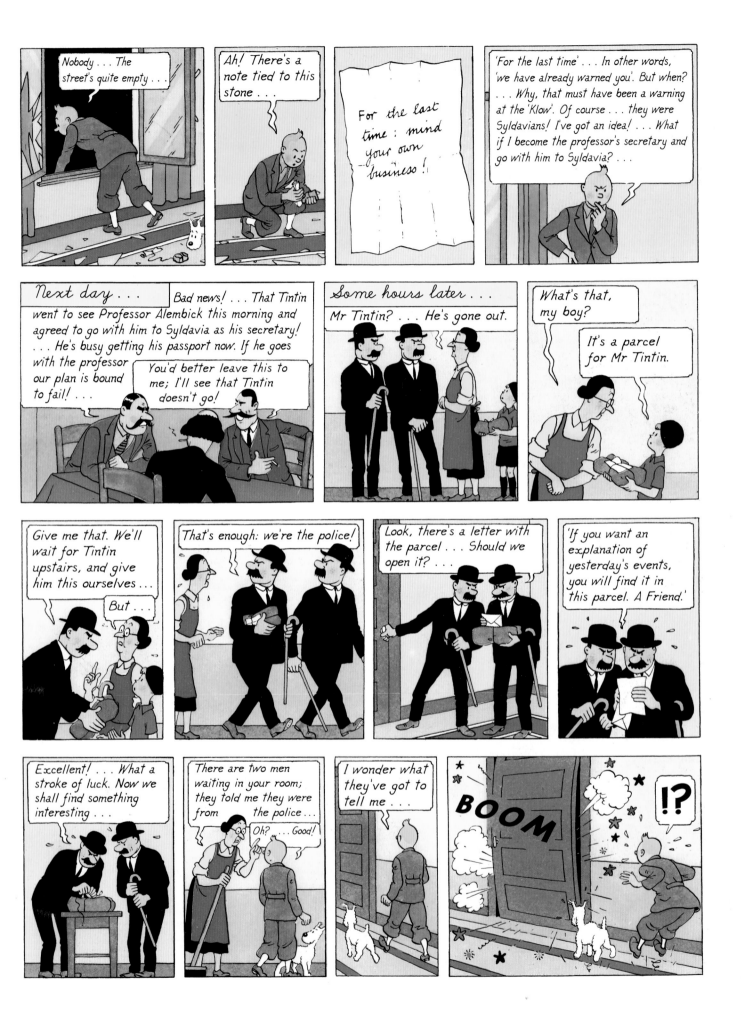

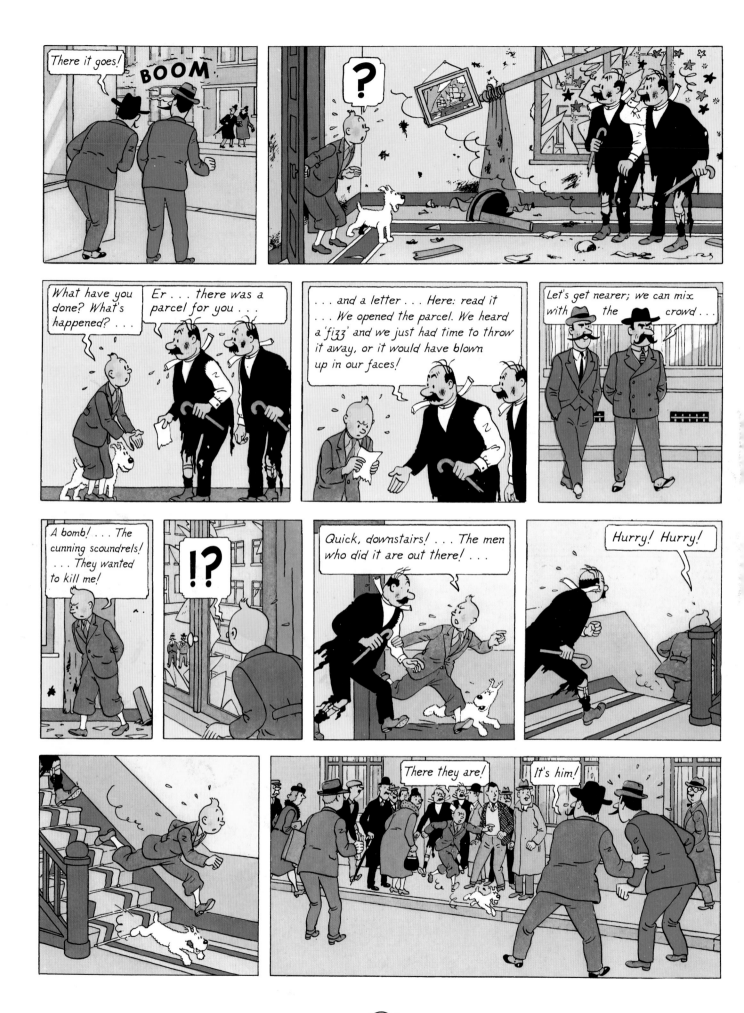

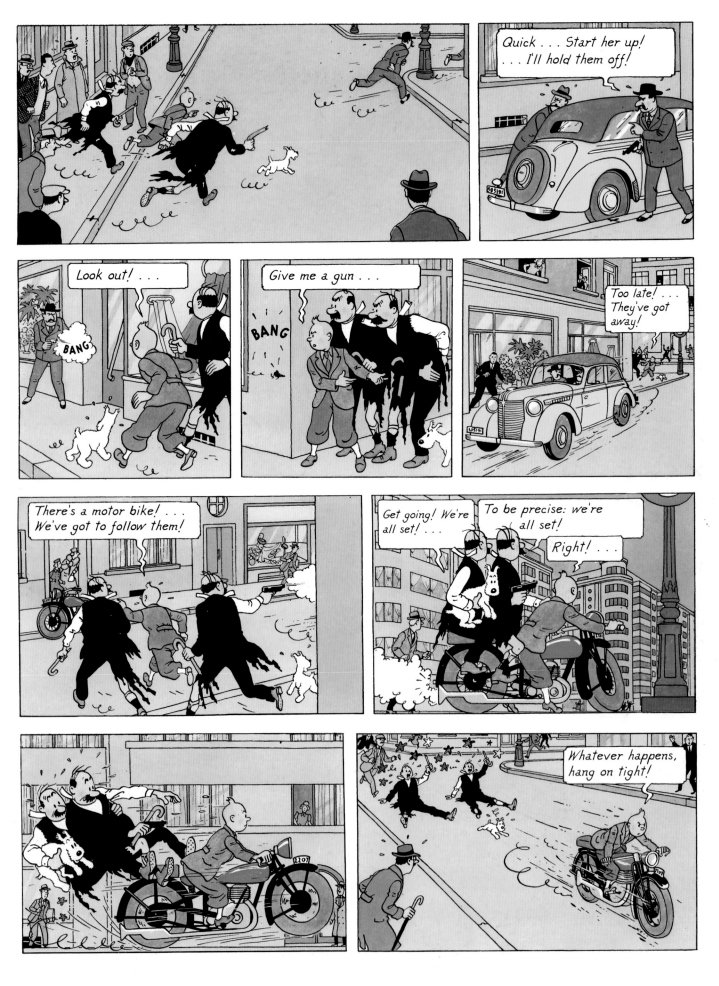

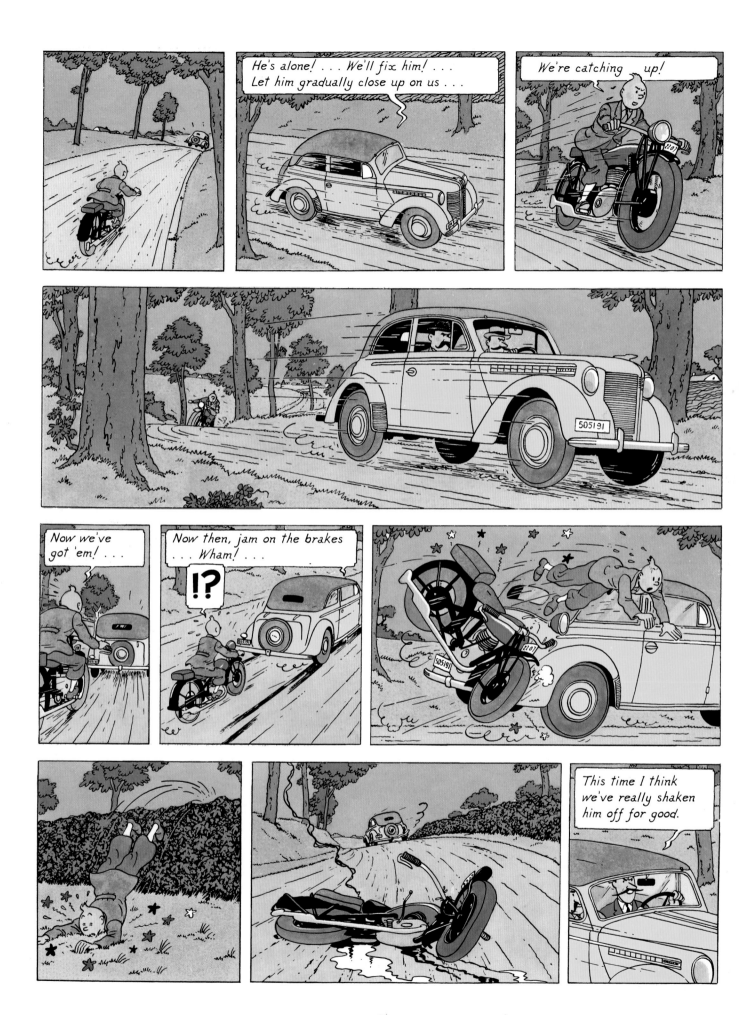

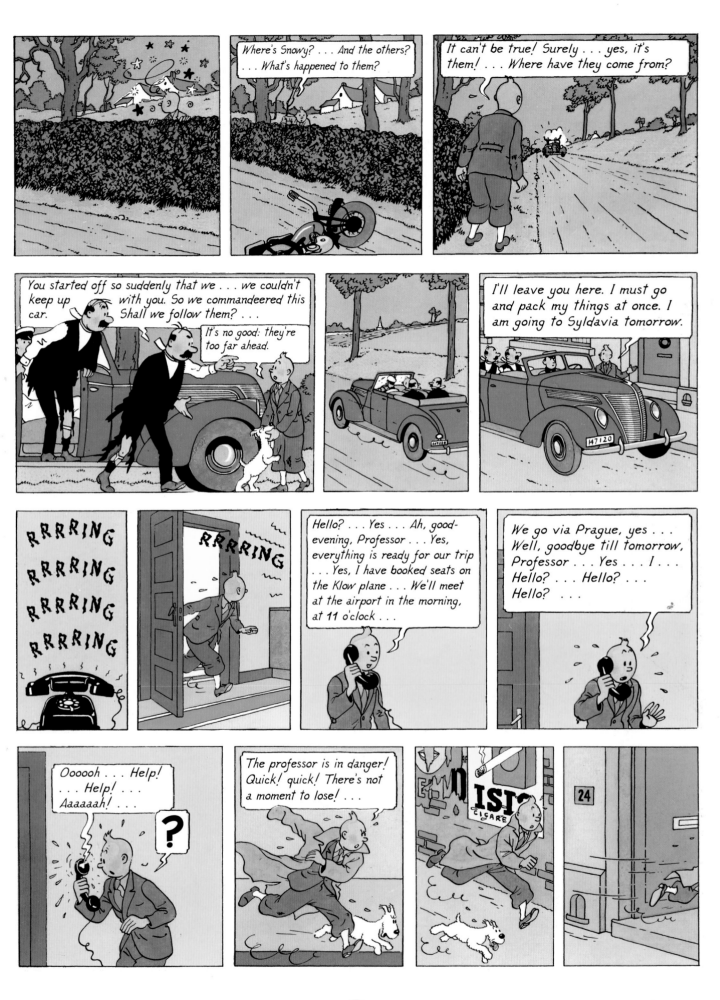

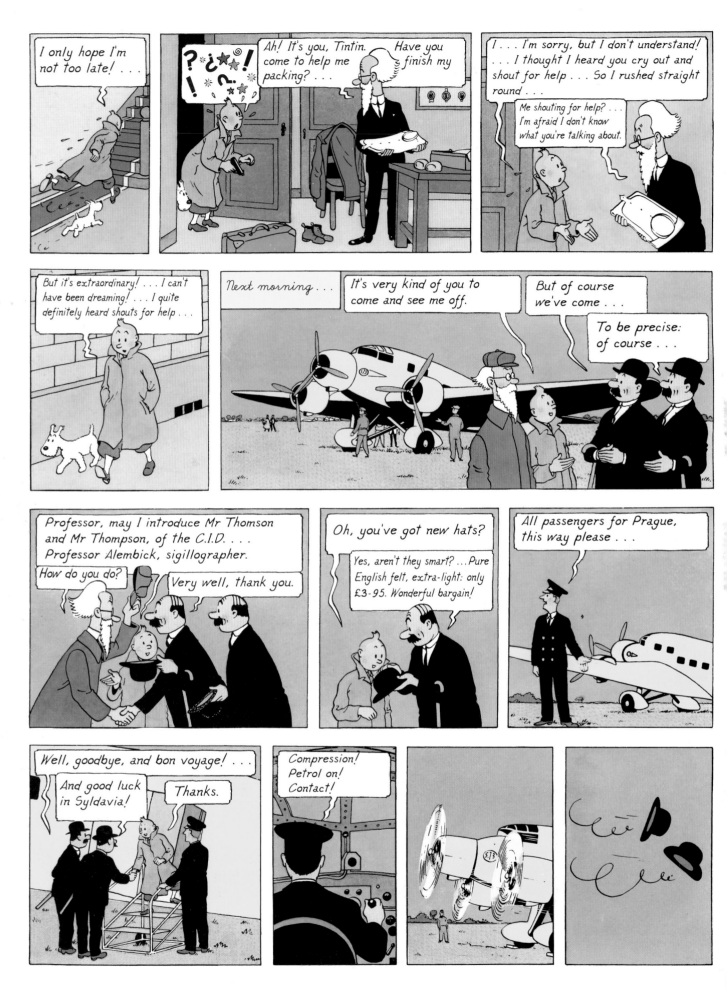

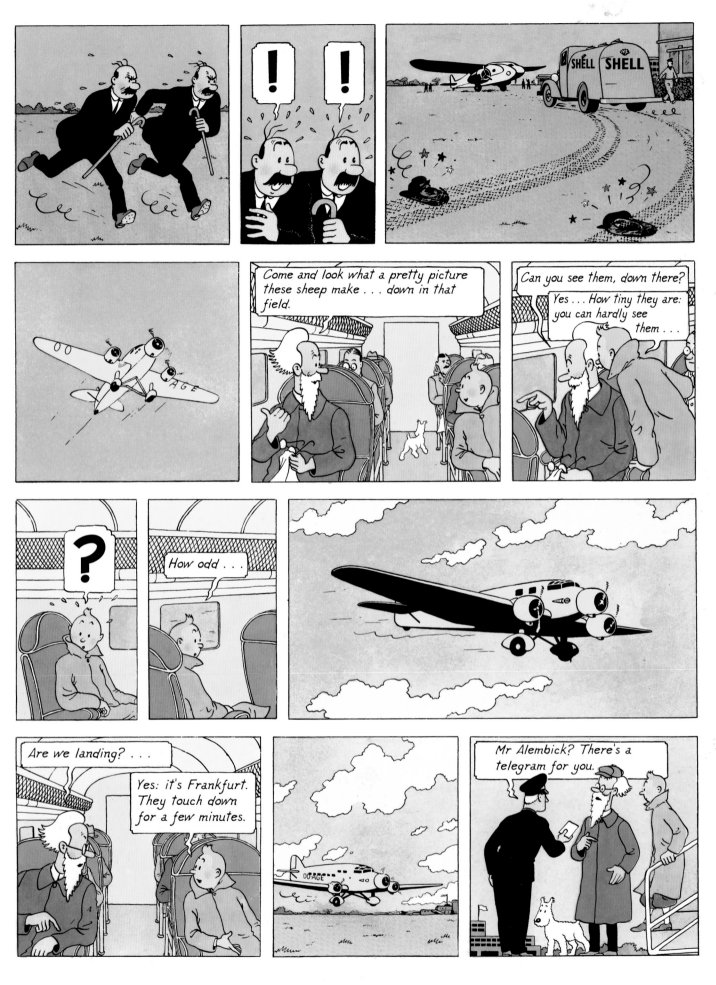

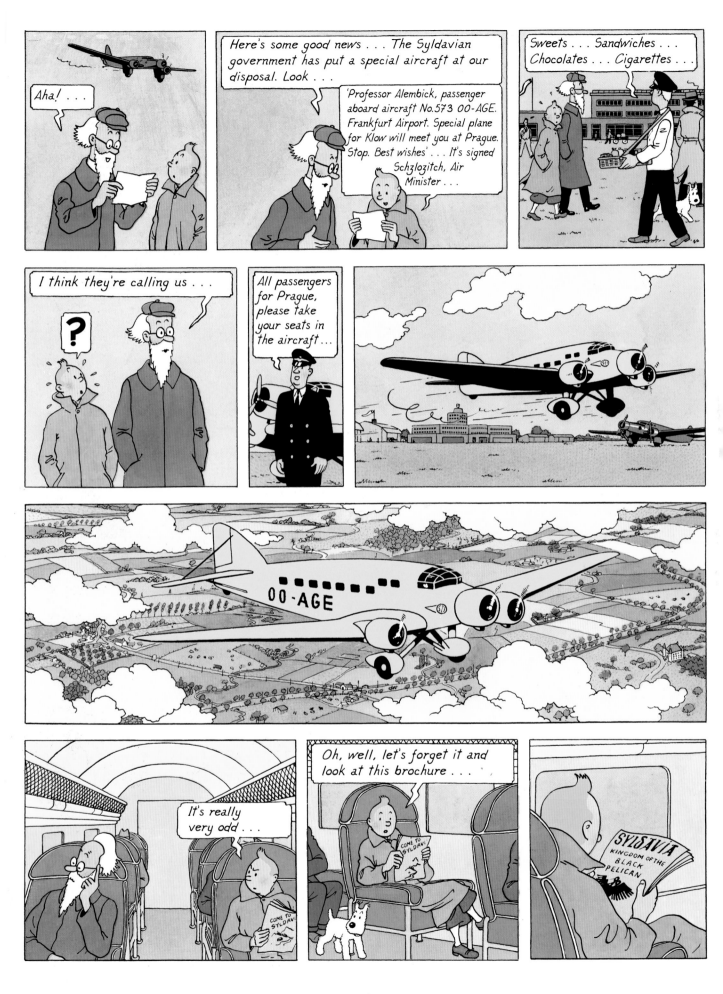

SYLDAVIA
THE KINGDOM OF THE BLACK PELICAN

MONG the many enchanting places which deservedly attract foreign visitors with a love for picturesque ceremony and colourful folklore, there is one small country which, although relatively unknown, surpasses many others in interest. Isolated until modern times because of its inaccessible position, this country is now served by a regular air-line network, which brings it within the reach of all who love unspoiled beauty, the proverbial hospitality of a peasant people, and the charm of medieval customs which still survive despite the march of progress.

This is Syldavia.

Syldavia is a small country in Eastern Europe, comprising two great valleys: those of the river Vladir, and its tributary, the Moltus. The rivers meet at Klow, the capital (122,000 inhabitants). These valleys are flanked by wide plateaux covered with forests, and are surrounded by high, snow-capped mountains. In the fertile Syldavian plains are cornlands and cattle pastures. The subsoil is rich in minerals of all kinds.

Numerous thermal and sulphur springs gush from the earth, the chief centres being at Klow (cardiac diseases) and Kragoniedin (rheumatic complaints).

The total population is estimated to be 642,000 inhabitants.

Syldavia exports wheat, mineral-water from Klow, firewood, horses and violinists.

HISTORY OF SYLDAVIA

Until the VIth century, Syldavia was inhabited by nomadic tribes of unknown origin.

Overrun by the Slavs in the VIth century, the country was conquered in the Xth century by the Turks, who drove the Slavs into the mountains and occupied the plains.

In 1127, Hveghi, leader of a Slav tribe, swooped down from the mountains at the head of a band of partisans and fell upon isolated Turkish villages, putting all who resisted him to the sword. Thus he rapidly became master of a large part of Syldavian territory.

A great battle took place in the valley of the Moltus near Zileheroum, the Turkish capital of Syldavia, between the Turkish army and Hveghi's irregulars.

Enfeebled by long inactivity and badly led by incompetent officers, the Turkish army put up little resistance and fled in disorder.

Having vanquished the Turks, Hveghi was elected king, and given the name Muskar, that is, The Brave (Muskh: 'brave' and Kar: 'king').

The capital, Zileheroum, was renamed Klow, that is, Freetown, (Kloho: 'to free', and Ow: 'town').

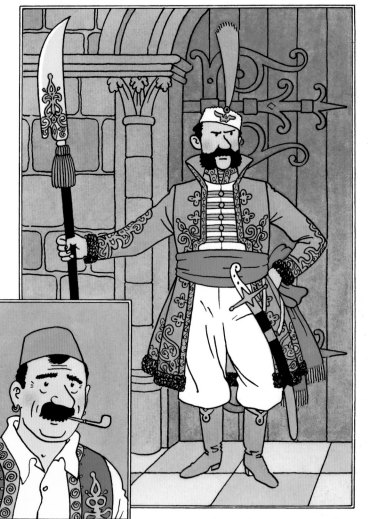

Guard at the Royal Treasure House, Klow

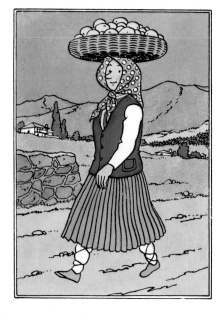

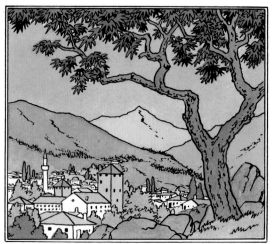

A typical fisherman from Dbrnouk (south coast of Syldavia)

◀ Syldavian peasant on her way to market

A view of Niedzdrow, in the Vladir valley ▶

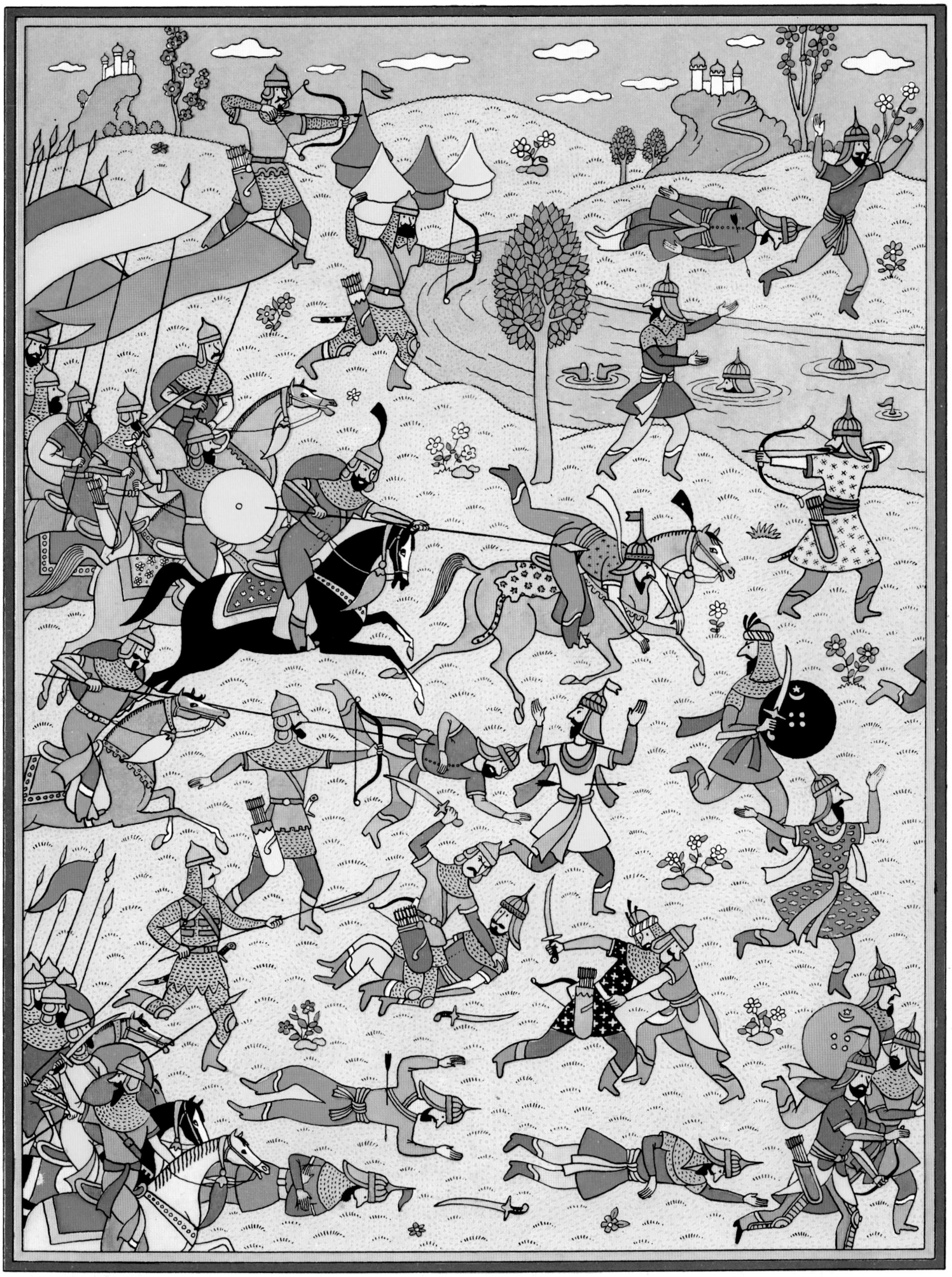

THE BATTLE OF ZILEHEROUM
After a XVth century miniature

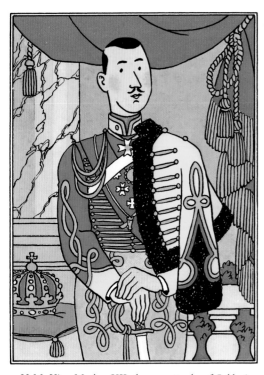

H.M. King Muskar XII, the present ruler of Syldavia in the uniform of Colonel of the Guards

Muskar was a wise king who lived at peace with his neighbours, and the country prospered. He died in 1168, mourned by all his subjects.

His eldest son succeeded to the throne with the title of Muskar II.

Unlike his father, Muskar II lacked authority and was unable to keep order in his kingdom. A period of anarchy replaced one of peaceful prosperity.

In the neighbouring state of Borduria the people observed Syldavia's decline, and their king profited by this opportunity to invade the country. Borduria annexed Syldavia in 1195.

For almost a century Syldavia groaned under the foreign yoke. In 1275 Baron Almaszout repeated the exploits of Hveghi by coming down from the hills and routing the Bordurians in less than six months.

He was proclaimed King in 1277, taking the name of Ottokar. He was, however, much less powerful than Muskar.

The barons who had helped him in the campaign against the Bordurians forced him to grant them a charter, based on the English Magna Carta signed by King John (Lackland). This marked the beginning of the feudal system in Syldavia.

Ottokar I of Syldavia should not be confused with the Ottakars (Premysls) who were Dukes, and later Kings, of Bohemia.

This period was noteworthy for the rise in power of the nobles, who fortified their castles and maintained bands of armed mercenaries, strong enough to oppose the King's forces.

But the true founder of the kingdom of Syldavia was Ottokar IV, who ascended the throne in 1370.

From the time of his accession he initiated widespread reforms. He raised a powerful army and subdued the arrogant nobles, confiscating their wealth.

He fostered the advancement of the arts, of letters, commerce and agriculture.

He united the whole nation and gave it that security, both at home and abroad, so necessary for the renewal of prosperity.

It was he who pronounced those famous words: '*Eih bennek, eih blavek*', which have become the motto of Syldavia.

The origin of this saying is as follows:

One day Baron Staszrvich, son of one of the dispossessed nobles whose lands had been forfeited to the crown, came before the sovereign and recklessly claimed the throne of Syldavia.

The King listened in silence, but when the presumptuous baron's speech ended with a demand that he deliver up his sceptre, the King rose and cried fiercely: 'Come and get it!'

Mad with rage, the young baron drew his sword, and before the retainers could intervene, fell upon the King.

The King stepped swiftly aside, and as his adversary passed him, carried forward by the impetus of his charge, Ottokar struck

him a blow on the head with the sceptre, laying him low and at the same time crying in Syldavian: '*Eih bennek, eih blavek!*', which can be said to mean: 'If you gather thistles, expect prickles'. And turning to his astonished court he said: '*Honi soit qui mal y pense!*'

Then, gazing intently at his sceptre, he addressed it in the following words: 'O Sceptre, thou has saved my life. Be henceforward the true symbol of Syldavian Kingship. Woe to the king who loses thee, for I declare that such a man shall be unworthy to rule thereafter.'

And from that time, every year on St. Vladimir's Day each successor of Ottokar IV has made a great ceremonial tour of his capital.

He bears in his hand the historic sceptre, without which he would lose the right to rule; as he passes, the people sing the famous anthem:

Syldavians unite!
Praise our King's might:
The Sceptre his right!

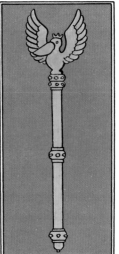

Right: The sceptre of Ottokar IV

Below: An illuminated page from 'The Memorable Deeds of Ottokar IV', a XIVth century manuscript

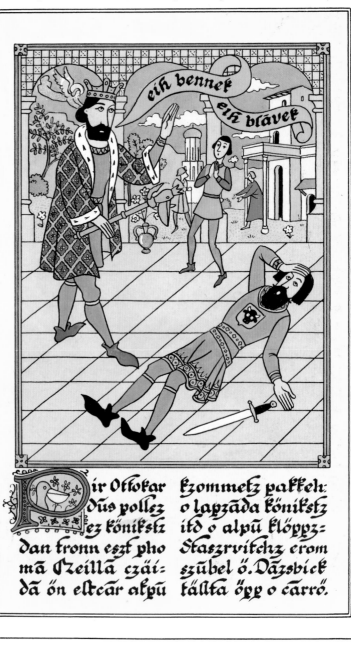

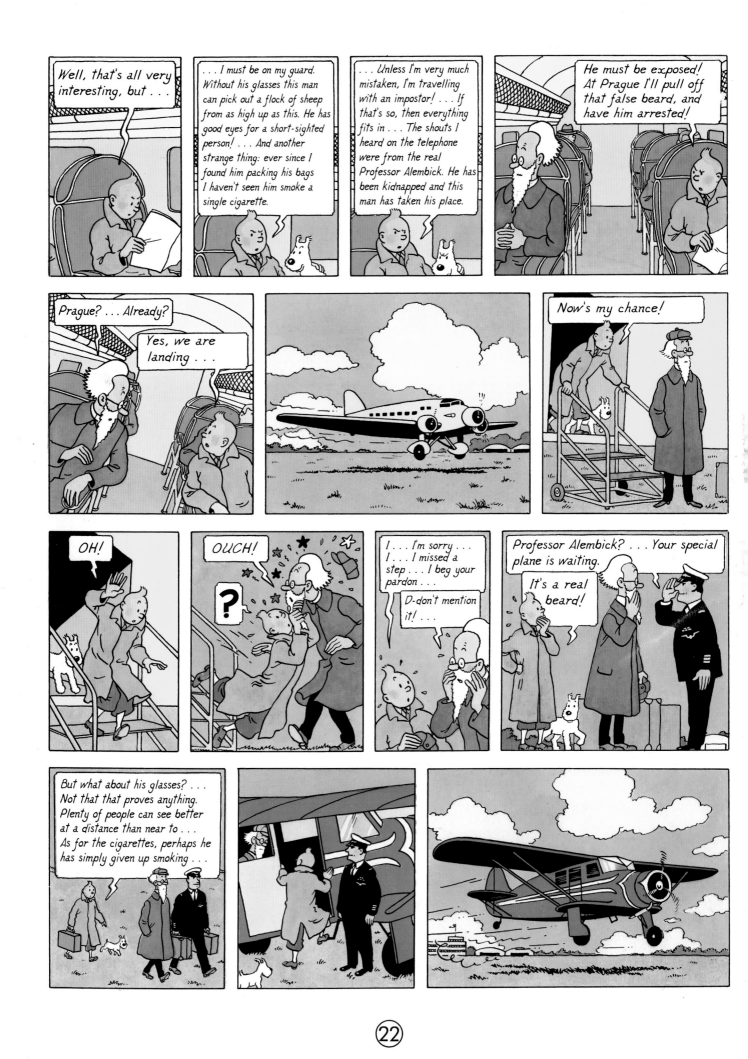

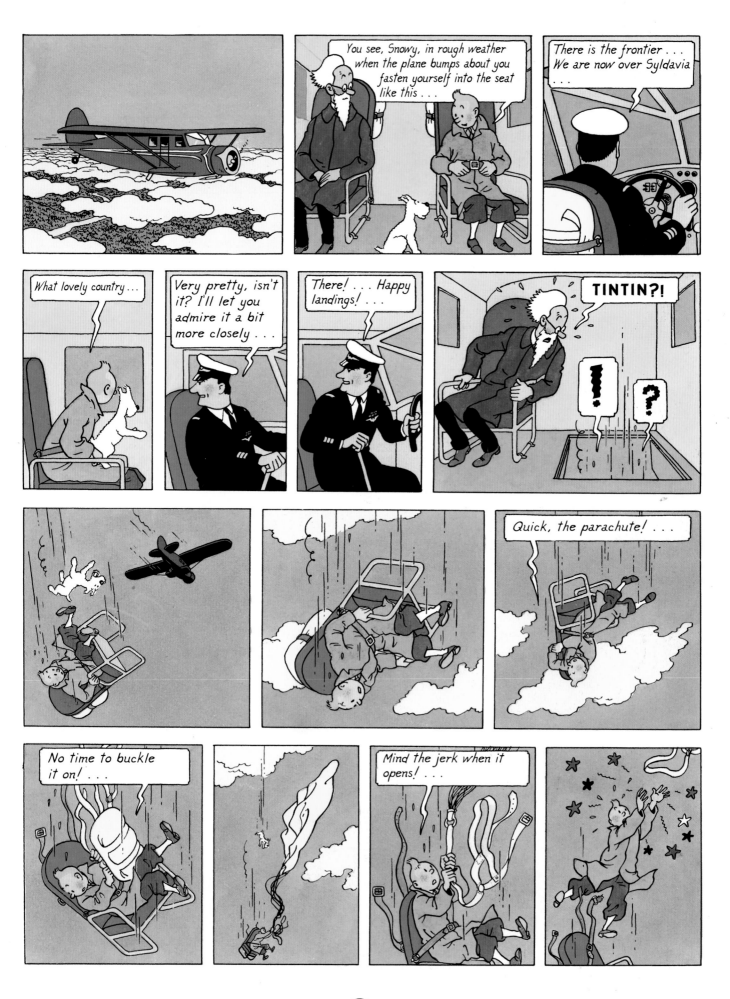

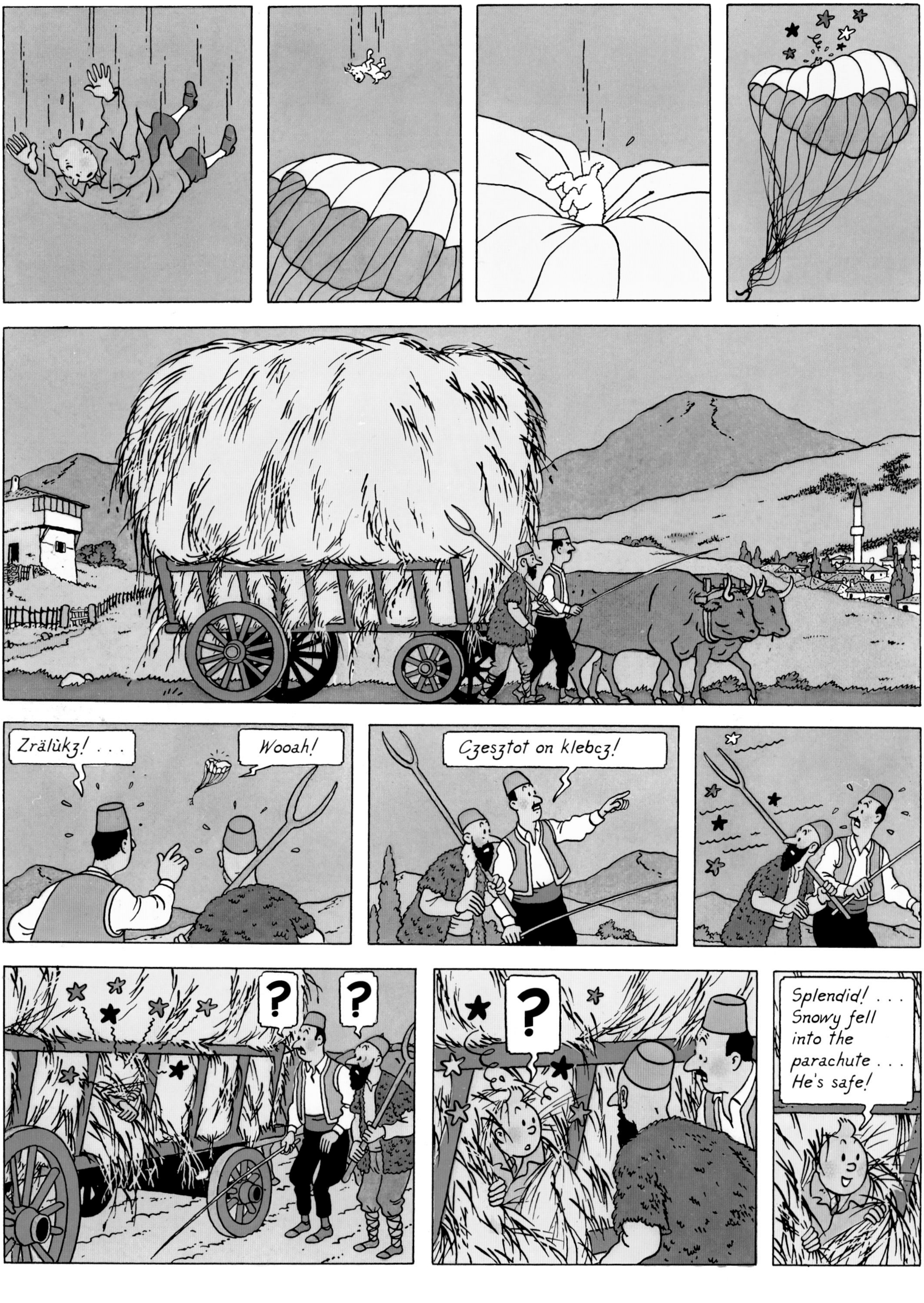
Zrälùkz! . . .
Wooah!
Czesztot on klebcz!
?
?
?
Splendid! . . . Snowy fell into the parachute . . . He's safe!

My aeroplane . . . BRRRR . . . I fell . . . Crash! . . . Into the straw . . .

Czestot wzryzkar nietz on vaghabontz! . . . Czestot bätczer yhzer kzömmetz noh dascz politzski? . . .

Snowy! Snowy!

Wooah! Wooah!

Kzommet micz omhz, noh dascz politzski!

Come with you to the police? . . . With pleasurski! . . . I've got a complaint to make!

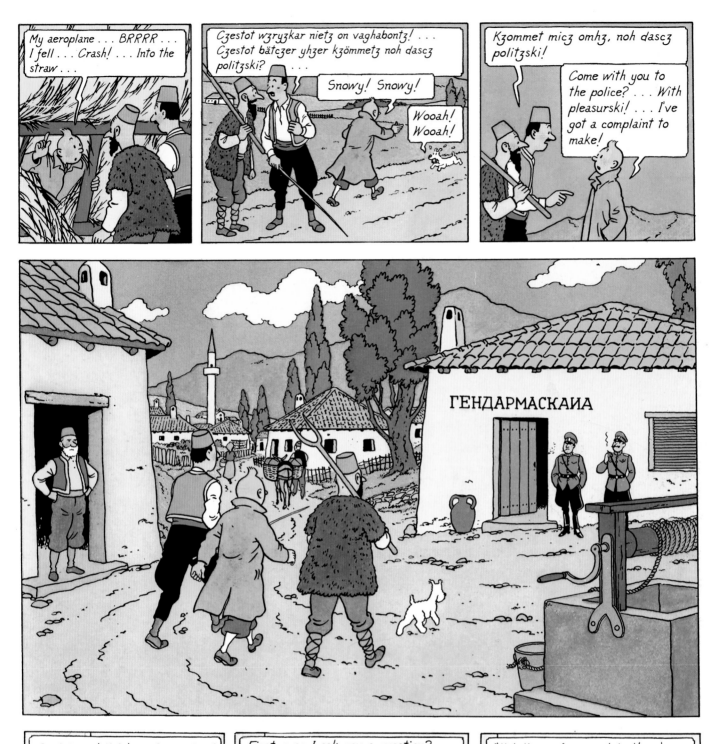

ГЕНДАРМАСКАИА

Captain, what I have to say is of the utmost importance . . . May I speak to you in private? . . .

Er . . . Yes . . . Leave us alone . . .

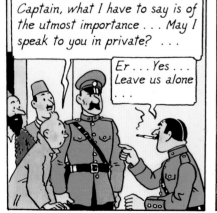

First, may I ask you a question? . . . I read in a brochure about Syldavia that if your King loses his sceptre he will be forced to abdicate. Is that true? . . .

As a matter of fact it is . . . But how does this concern you?

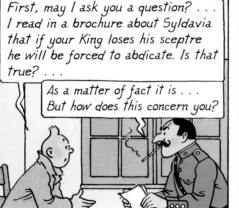

I'll tell you. I am certain there's a conspiracy against King Muskar XII, and that certain people will try to steal the sceptre from him!

What's that you say? . . . What makes you imagine such a thing?

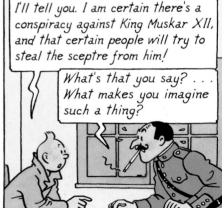

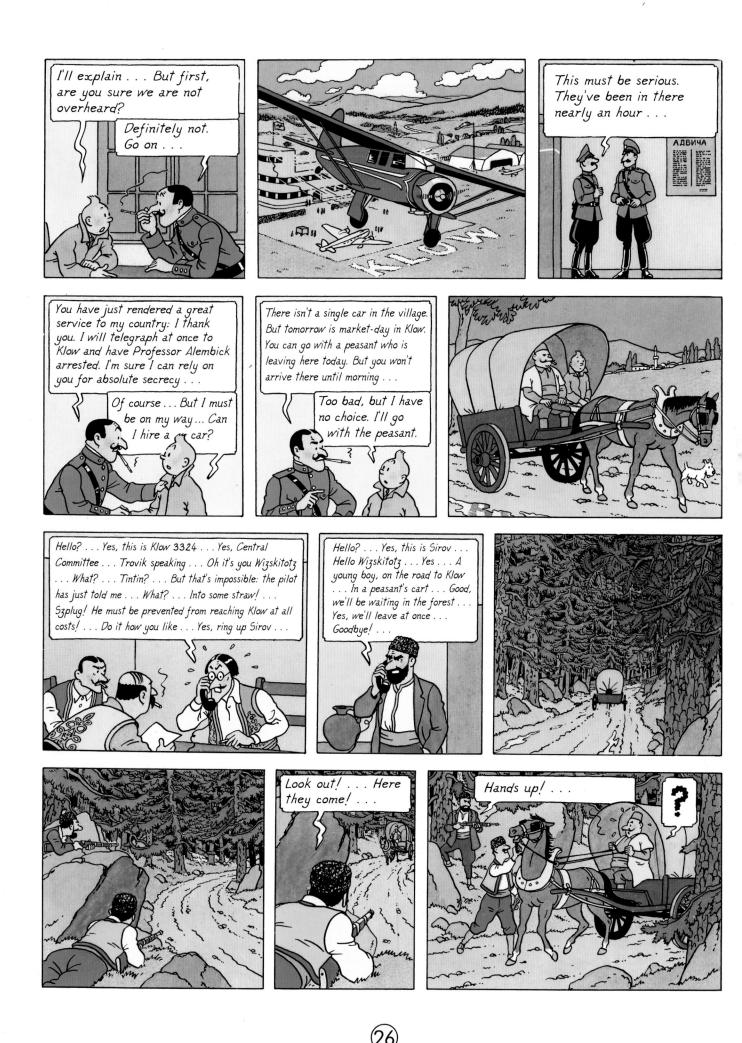

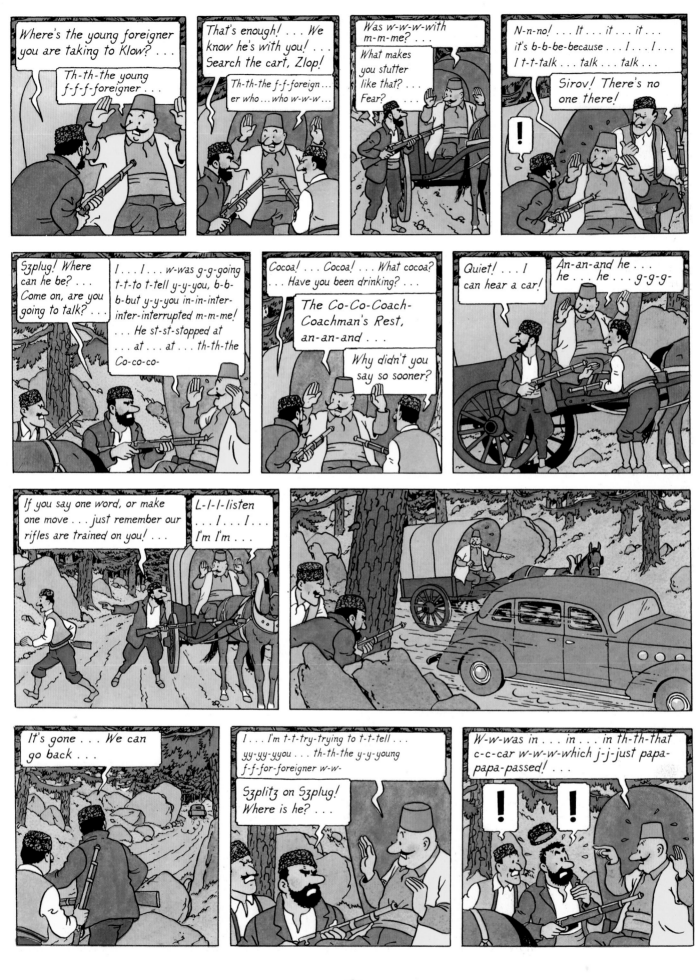

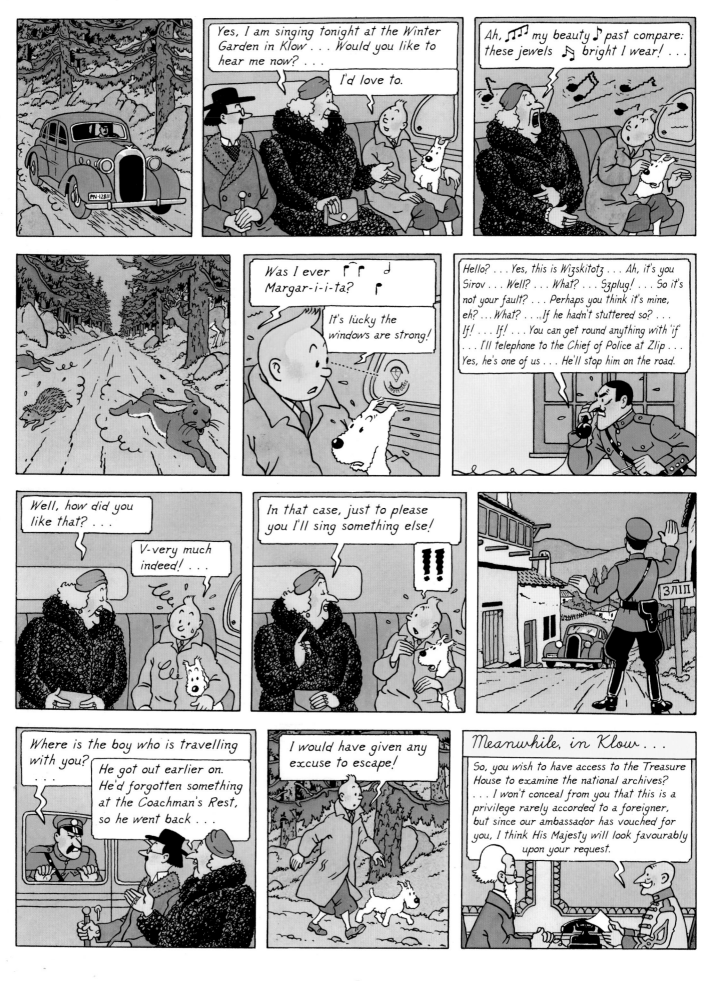

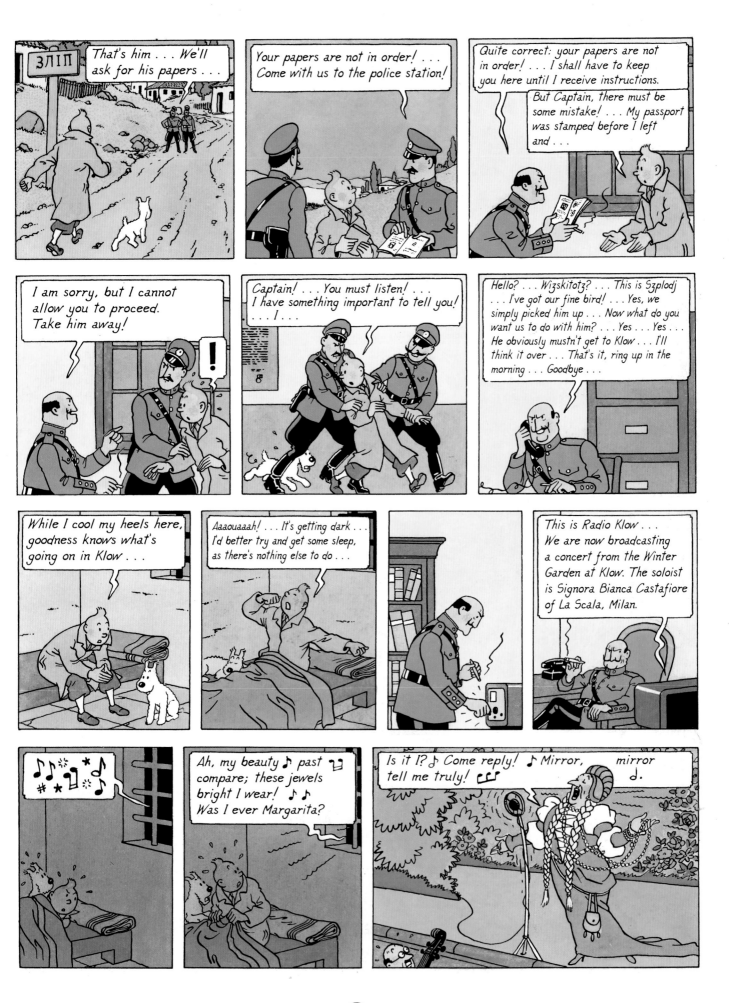

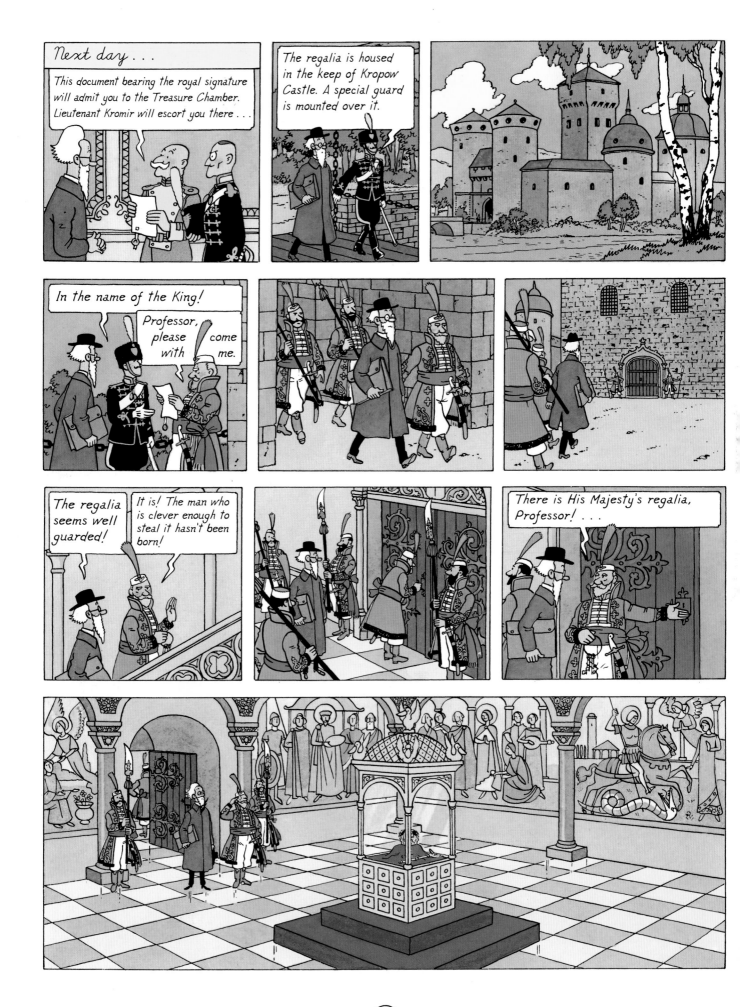

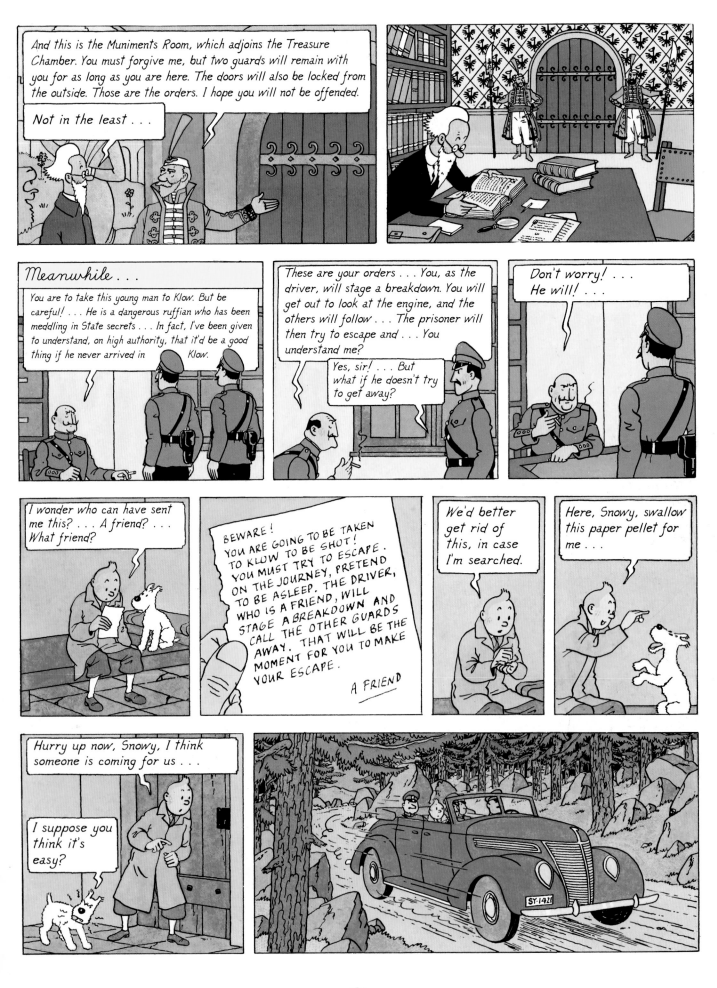

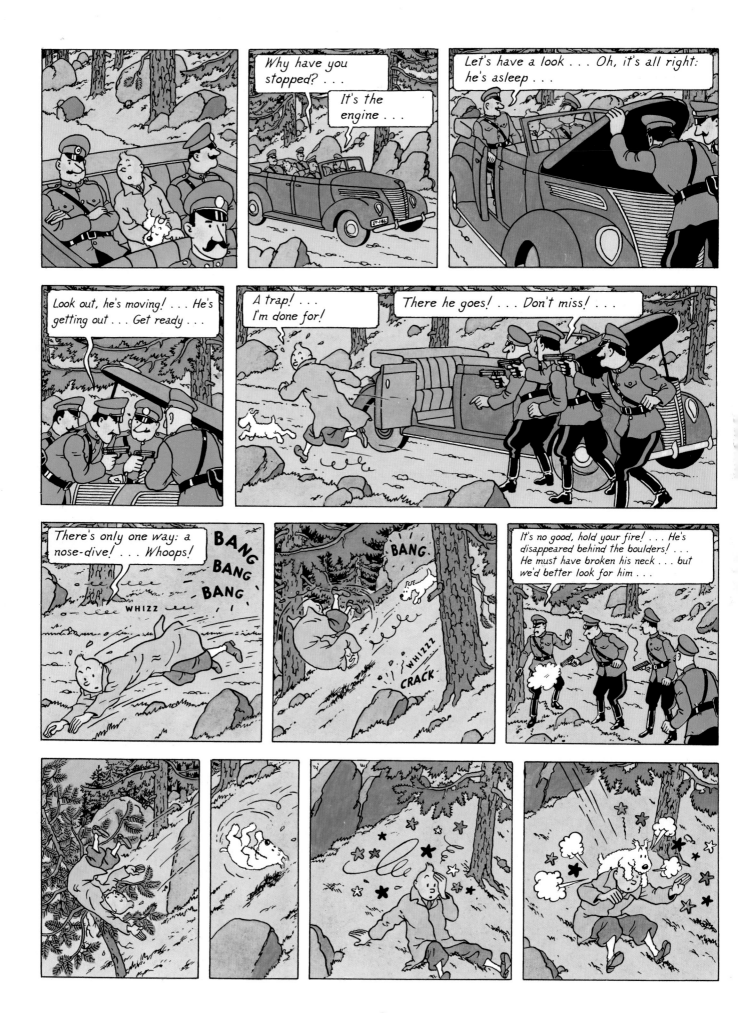

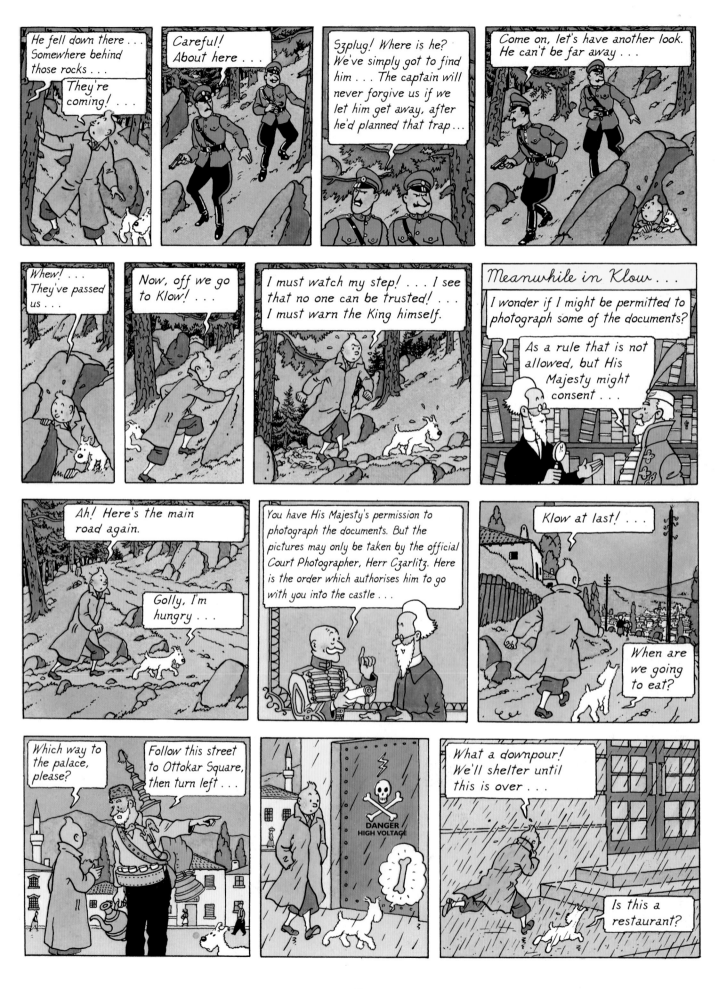

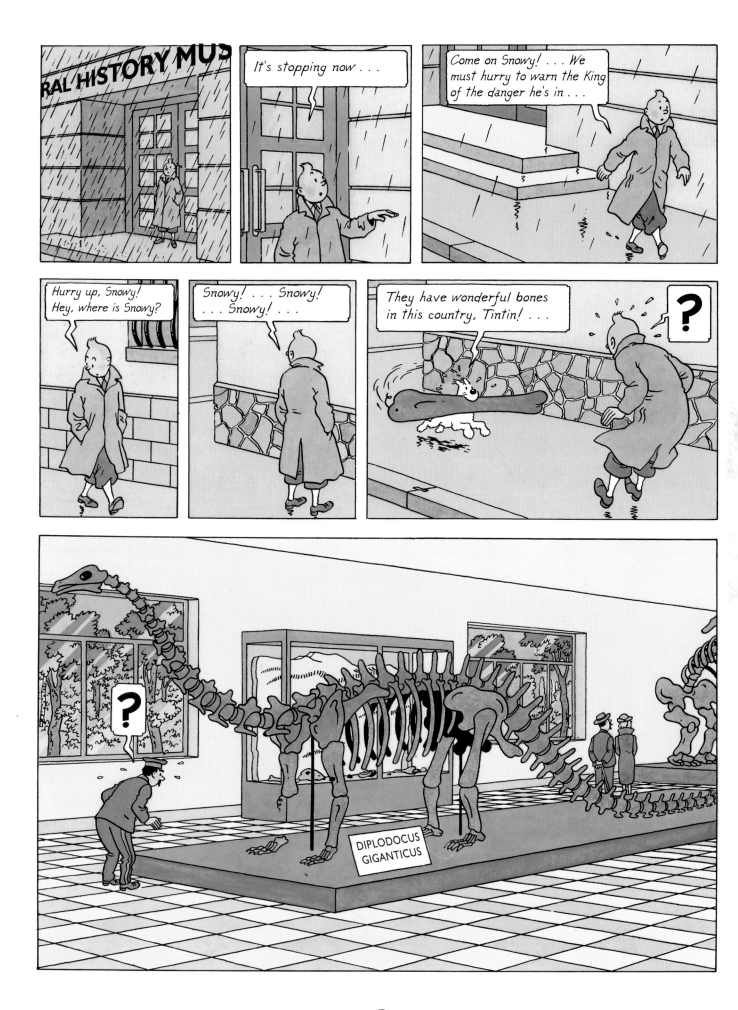

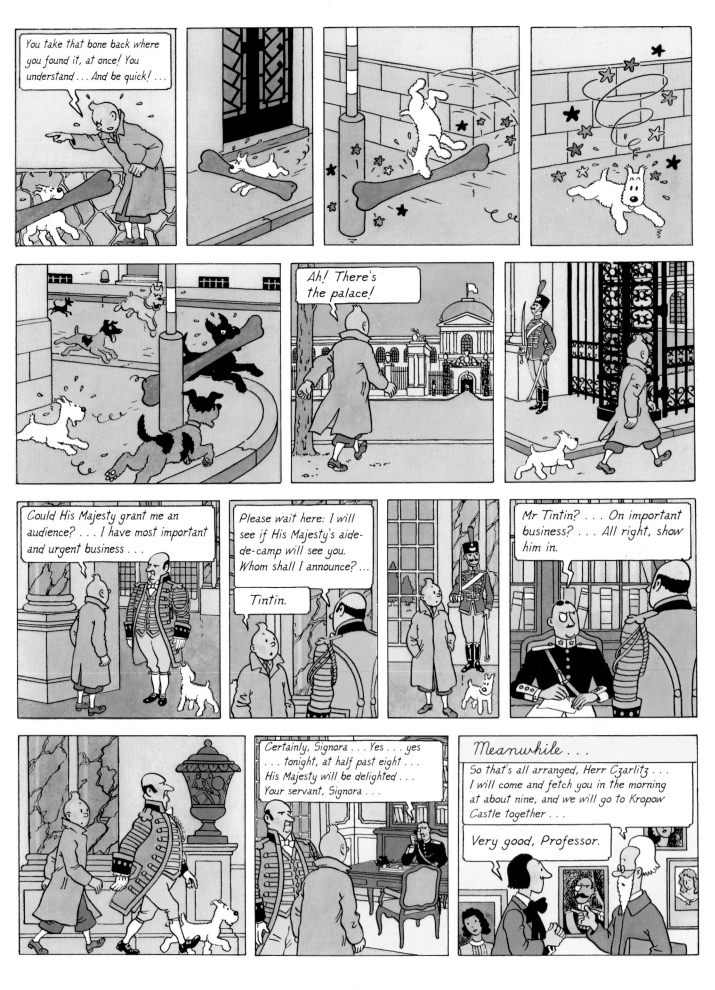

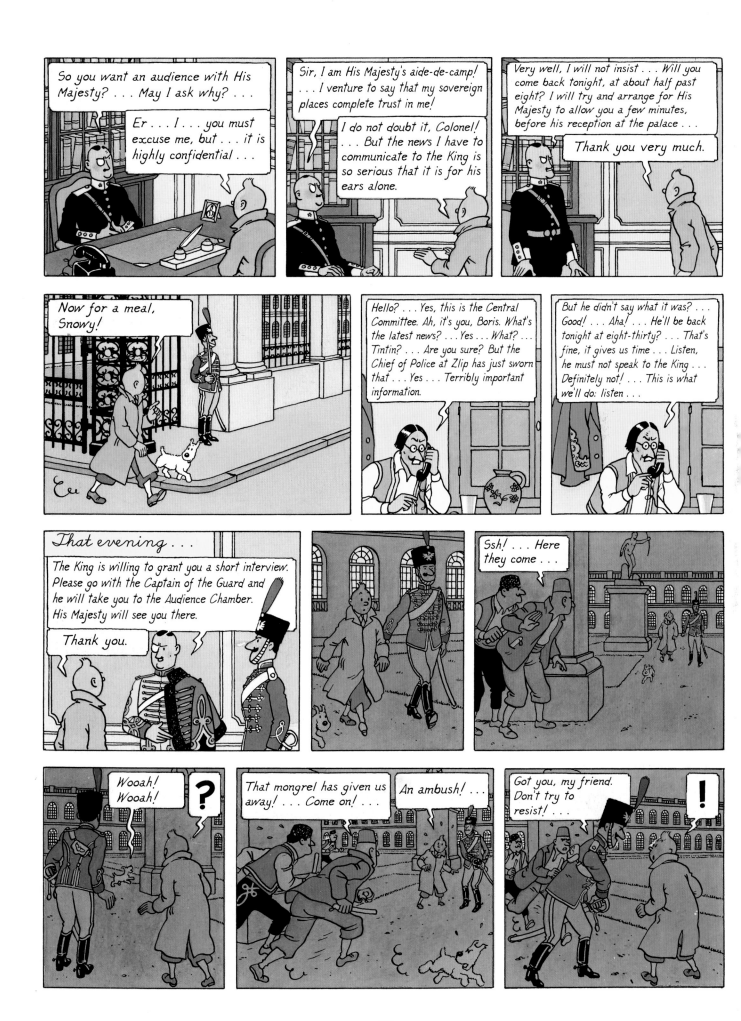

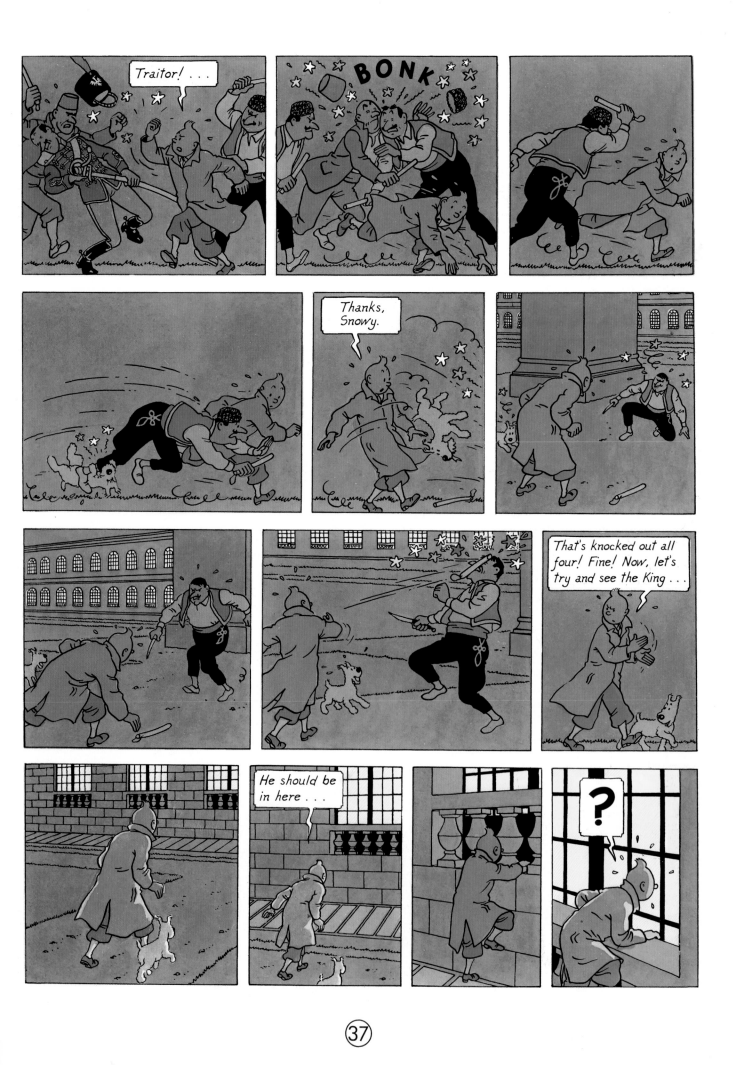

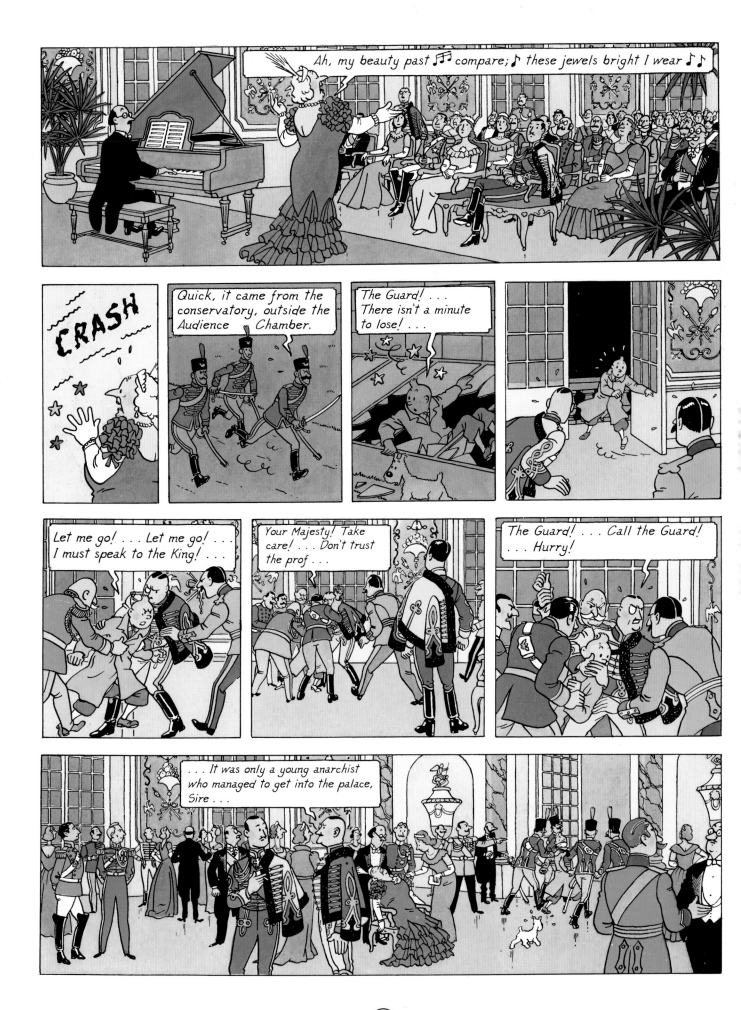

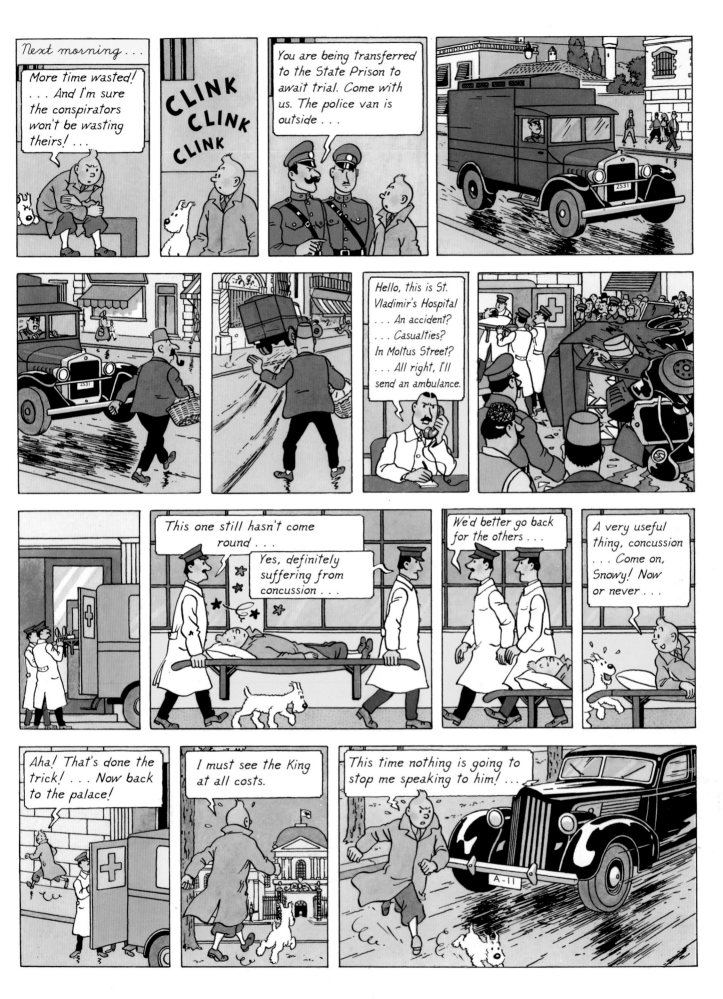

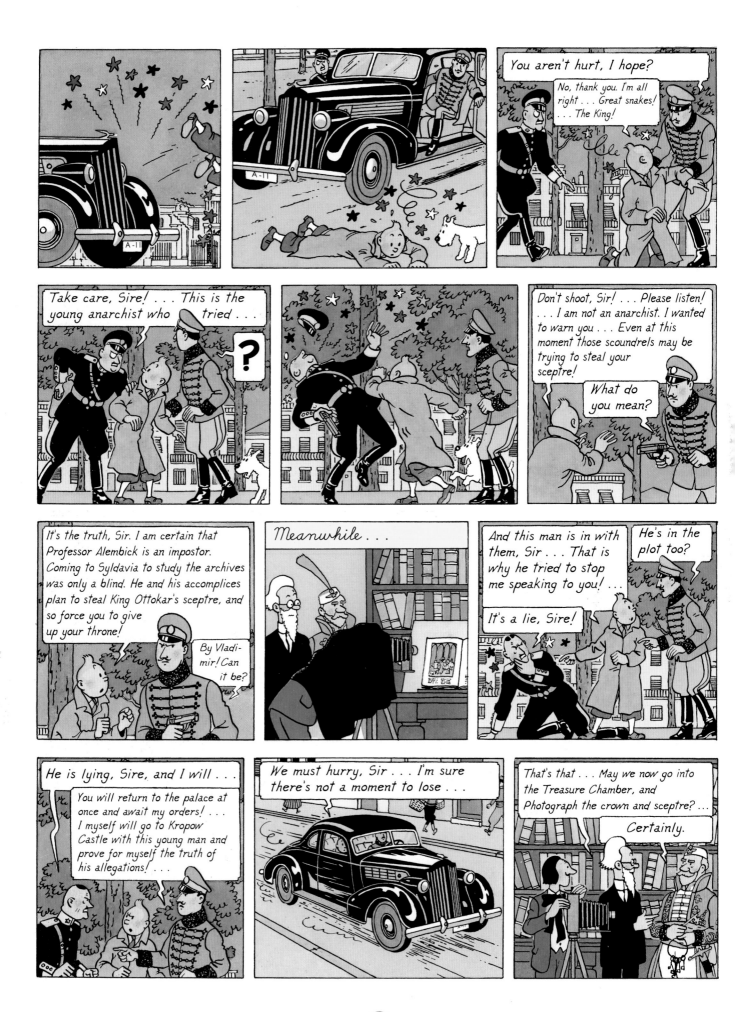

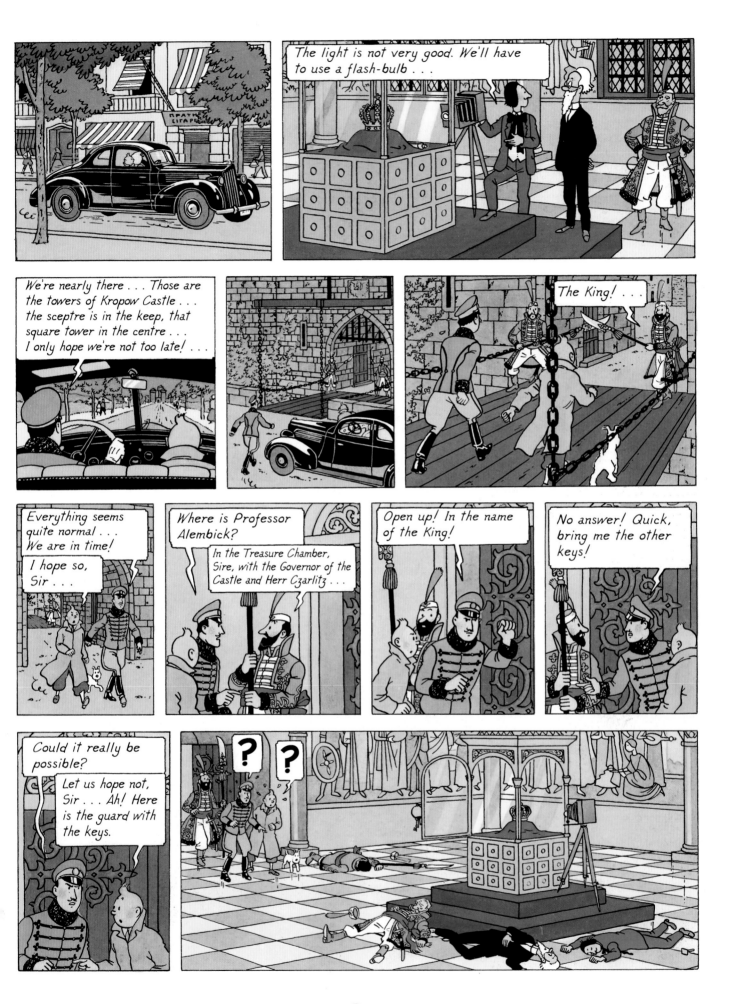

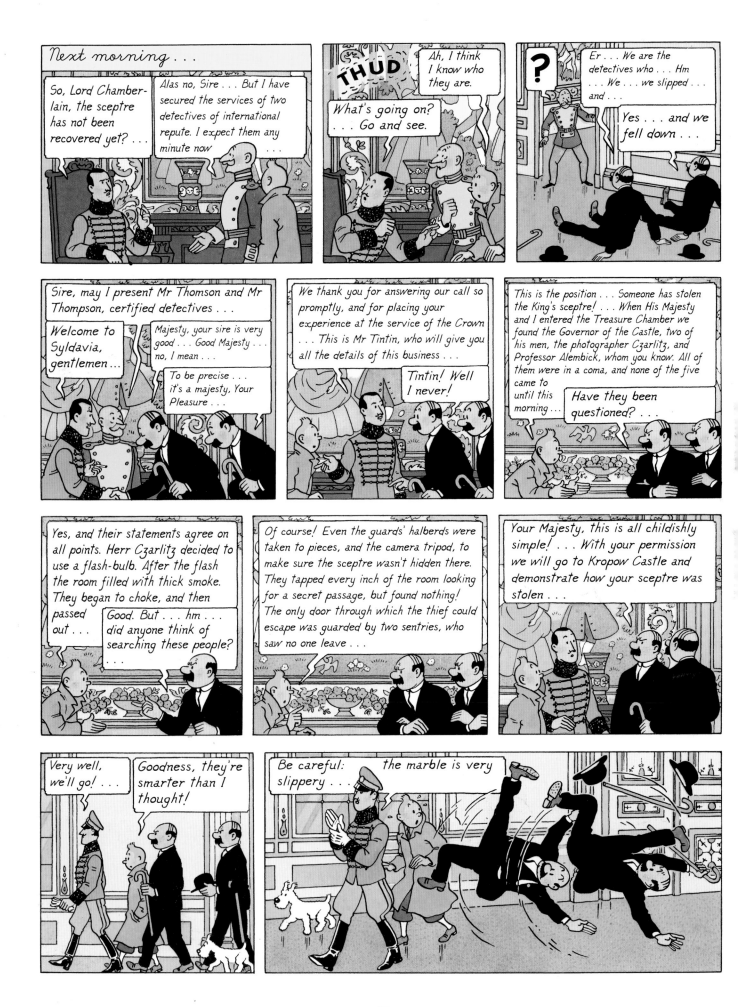

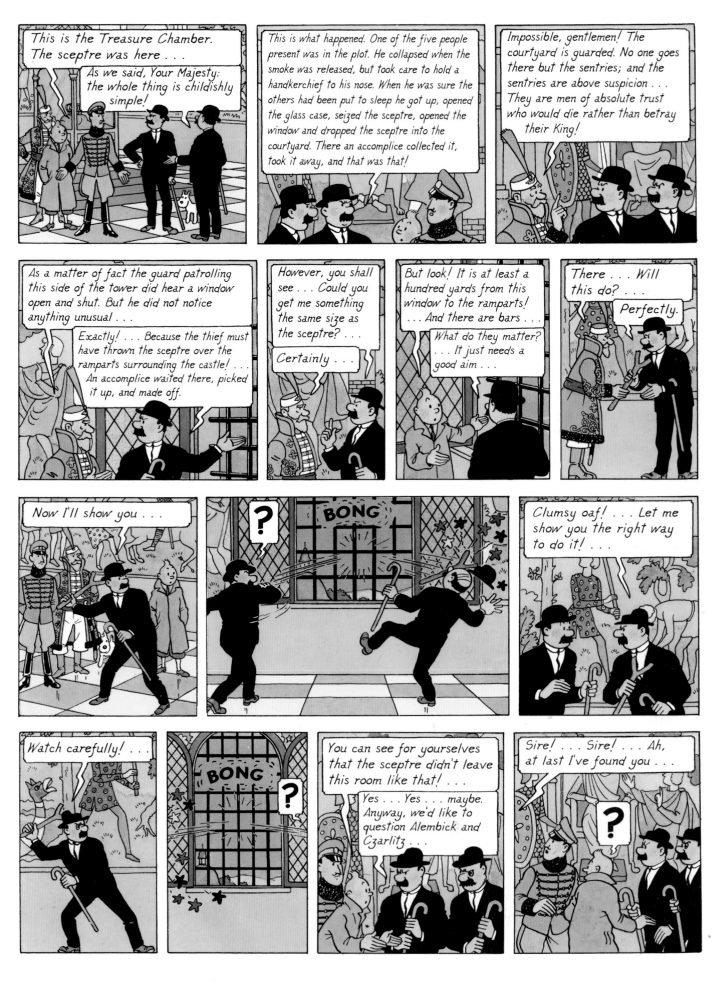

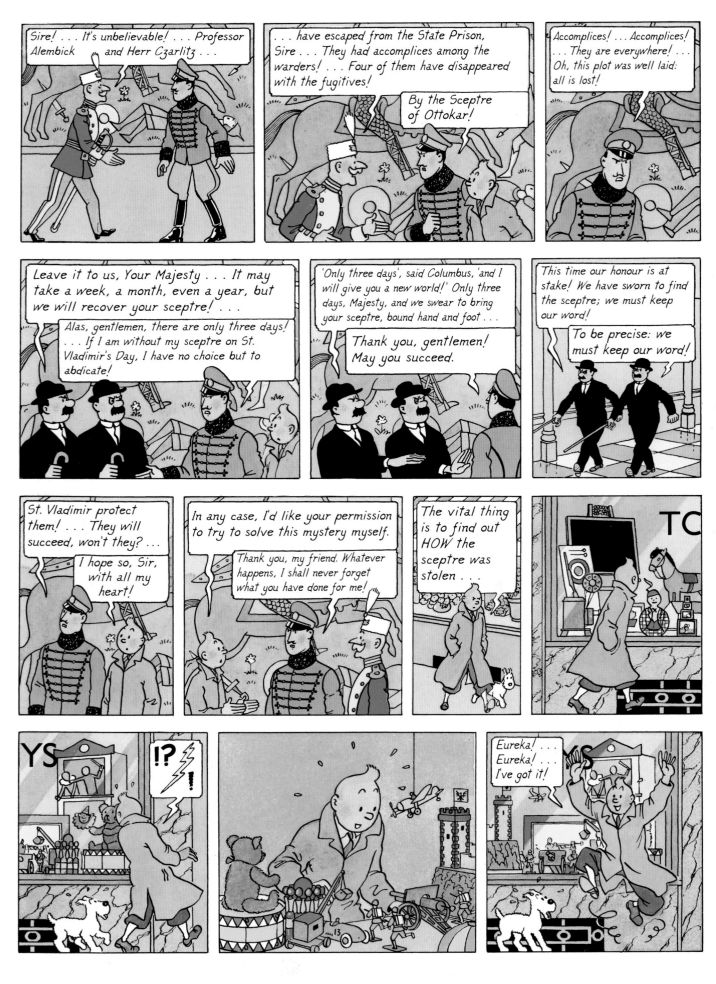

Sire! . . . It's unbelievable! . . . Professor Alembick and Herr Czarlitz . . .

. . . have escaped from the State Prison, Sire . . . They had accomplices among the warders! . . . Four of them have disappeared with the fugitives!

By the Sceptre of Ottokar!

Accomplices! . . . Accomplices! . . . They are everywhere! . . . Oh, this plot was well laid: all is lost!

Leave it to us, Your Majesty . . . It may take a week, a month, even a year, but we will recover your sceptre! . . .

Alas, gentlemen, there are only three days! . . . If I am without my sceptre on St. Vladimir's Day, I have no choice but to abdicate!

'Only three days', said Columbus, 'and I will give you a new world!' Only three days, Majesty, and we swear to bring your sceptre, bound hand and foot . . .

Thank you, gentlemen! May you succeed.

This time our honour is at stake! We have sworn to find the sceptre; we must keep our word!

To be precise: we must keep our word!

St. Vladimir protect them! . . . They will succeed, won't they? . . .

I hope so, Sir, with all my heart!

In any case, I'd like your permission to try to solve this mystery myself.

Thank you, my friend. Whatever happens, I shall never forget what you have done for me!

The vital thing is to find out HOW the sceptre was stolen . . .

!?

Eureka! . . . Eureka! . . . I've got it!

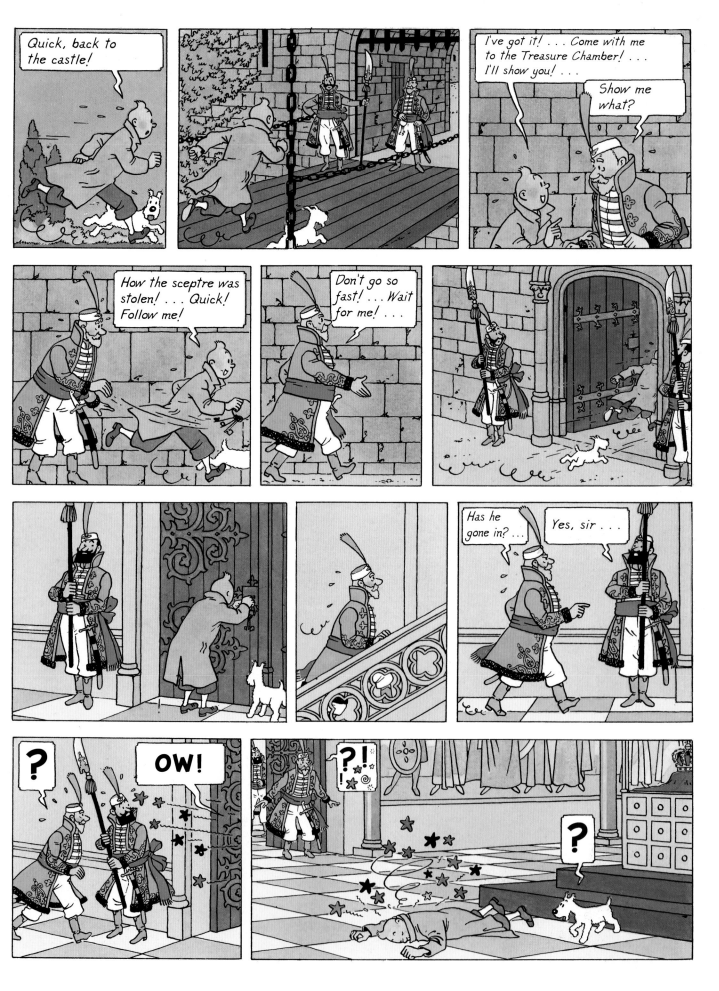

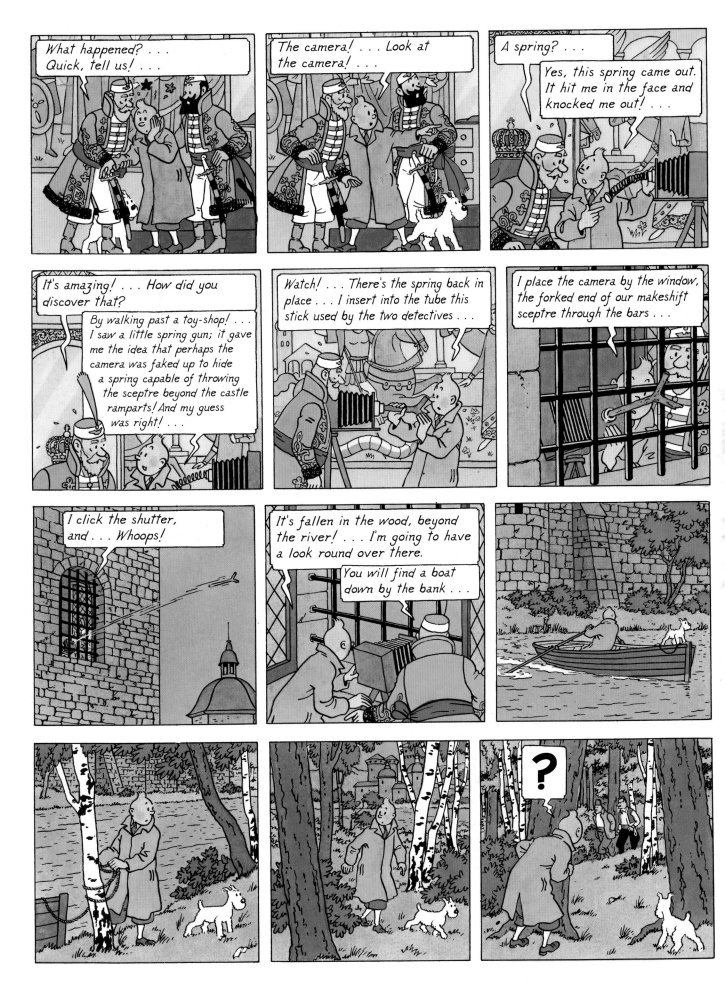

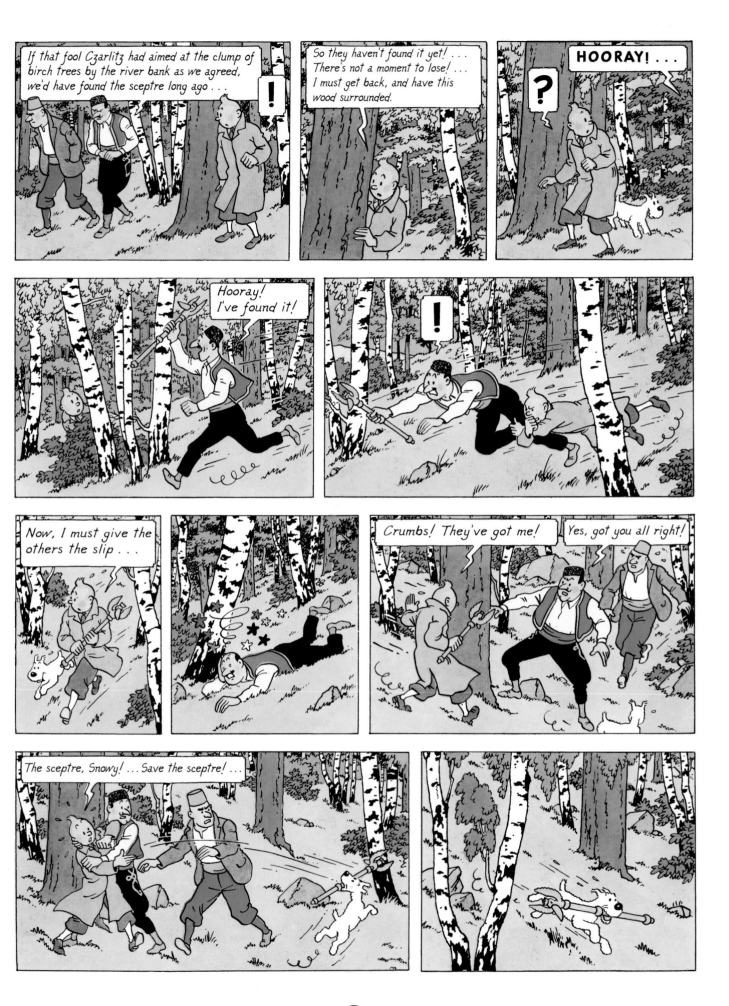

47

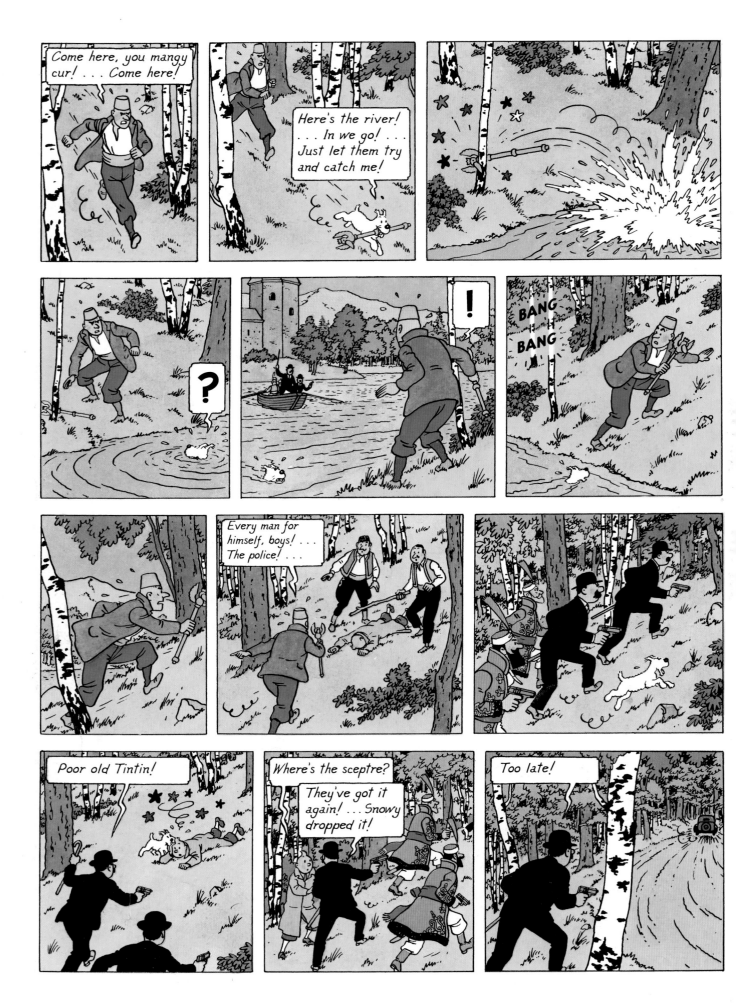

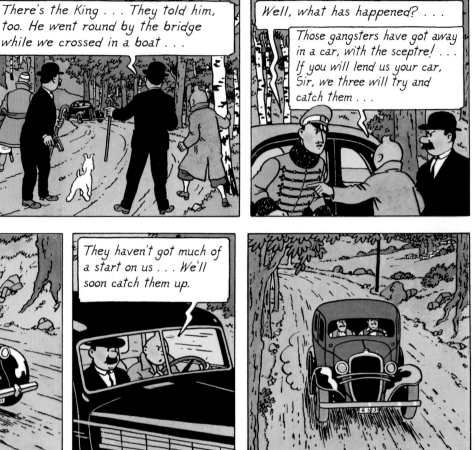

How did you know I was here?

When we went back to the castle they told us you had crossed the river . . .

There's the King . . . They told him, too. He went round by the bridge while we crossed in a boat . . .

Well, what has happened? . . .

Those gangsters have got away in a car, with the sceptre! . . . If you will lend us your car, Sir, we three will try and catch them . . .

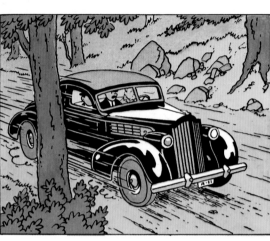

They haven't got much of a start on us . . . We'll soon catch them up.

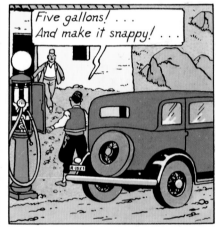

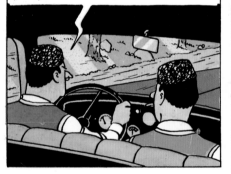

We're almost out of petrol . . . We'll have to stop at the first pump we come to . . .

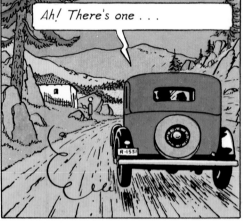

Ah! There's one . . .

Five gallons! . . . And make it snappy! . . .

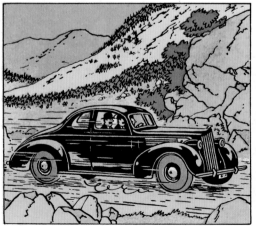

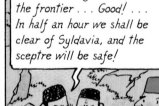

Another twenty miles to the frontier . . . Good! . . . In half an hour we shall be clear of Syldavia, and the sceptre will be safe!

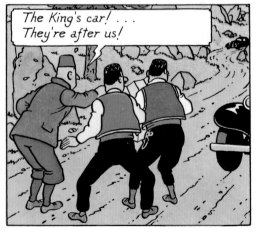

The King's car! . . . They're after us!

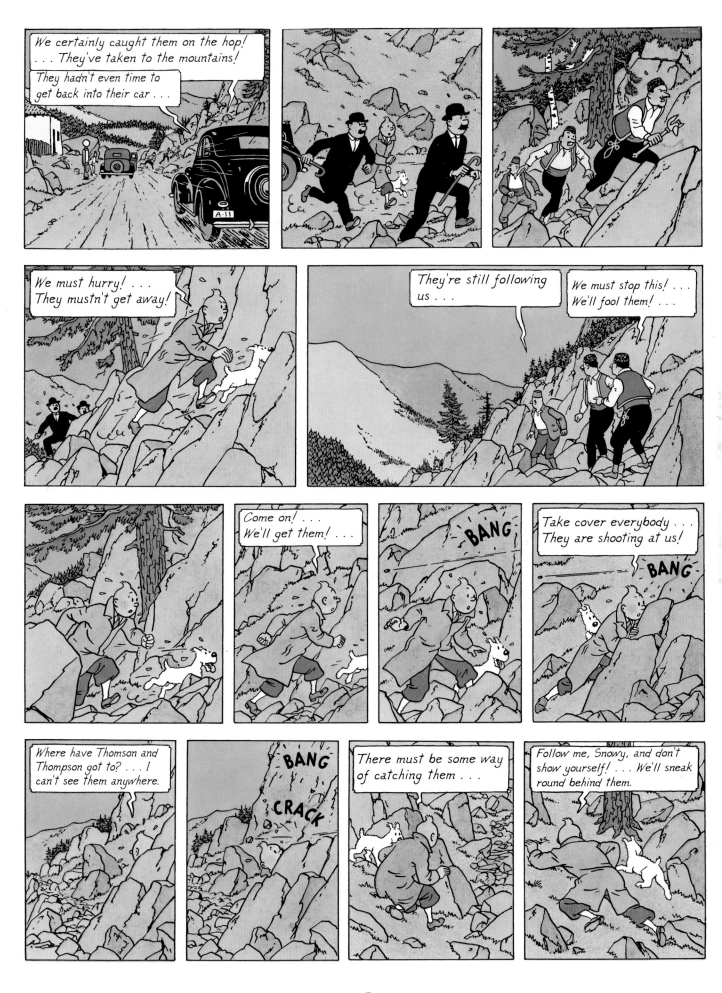

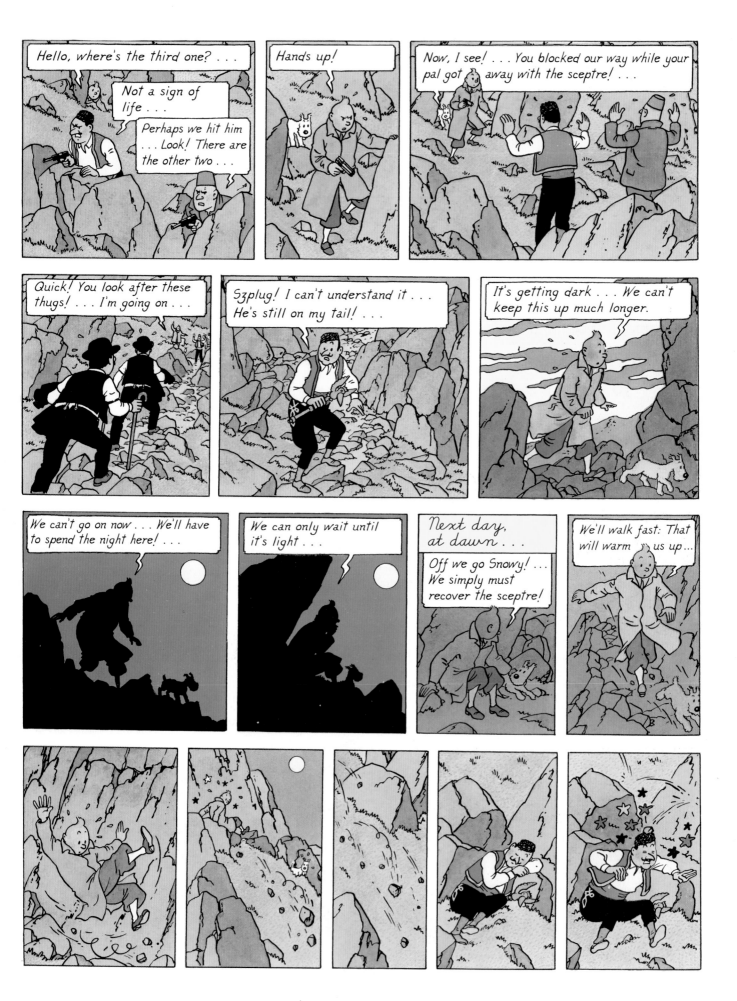

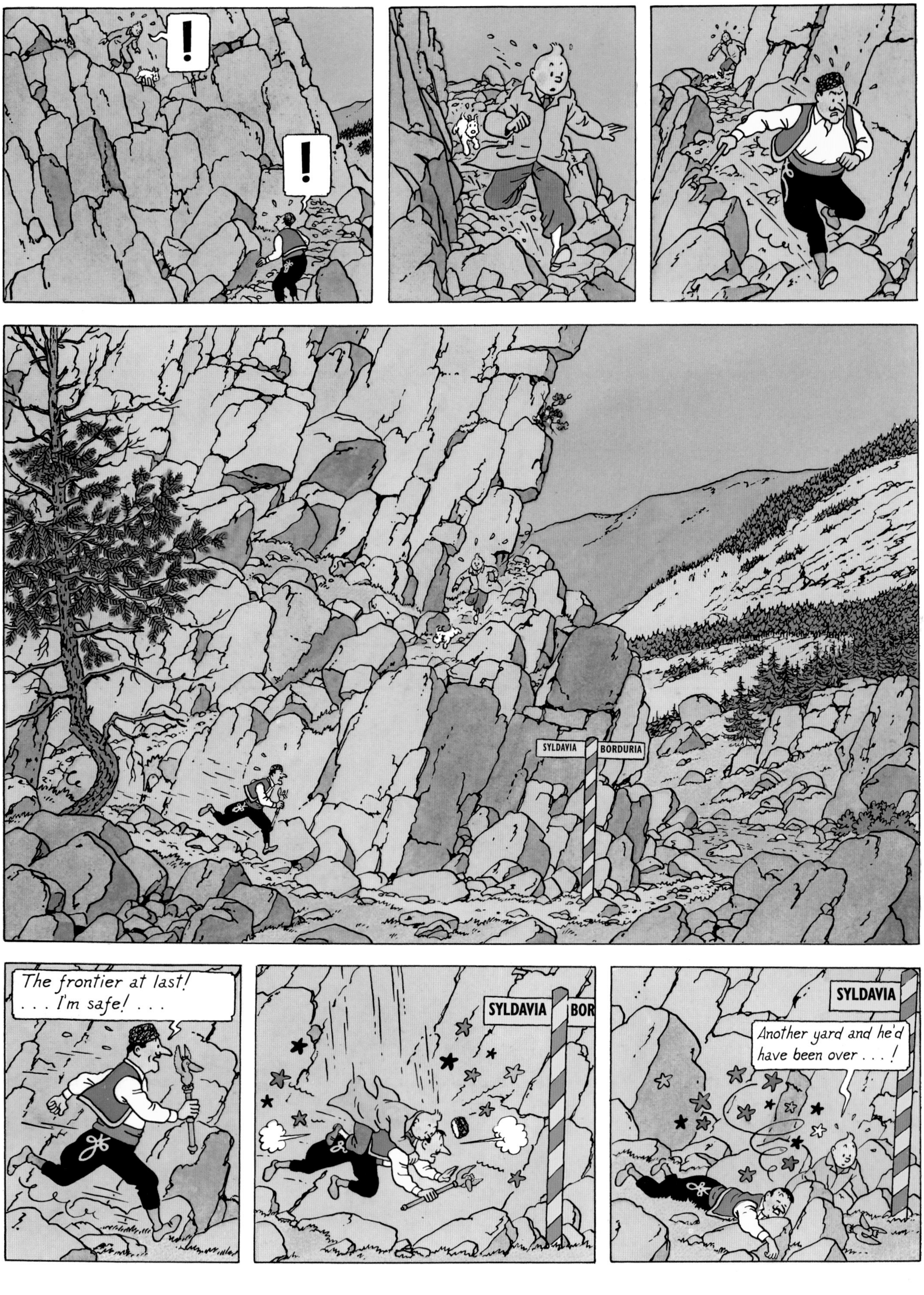
!
!
SYLDAVIA
BORDURIA
The frontier at last! . . . I'm safe! . . .
SYLDAVIA
BOR
SYLDAVIA
Another yard and he'd have been over . . . !

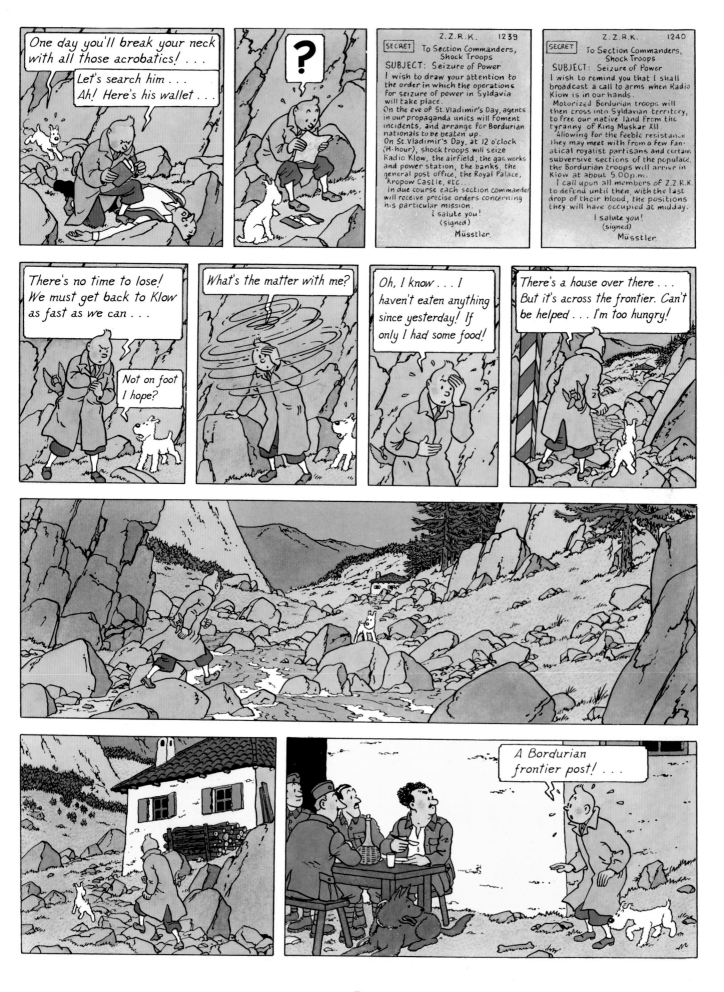

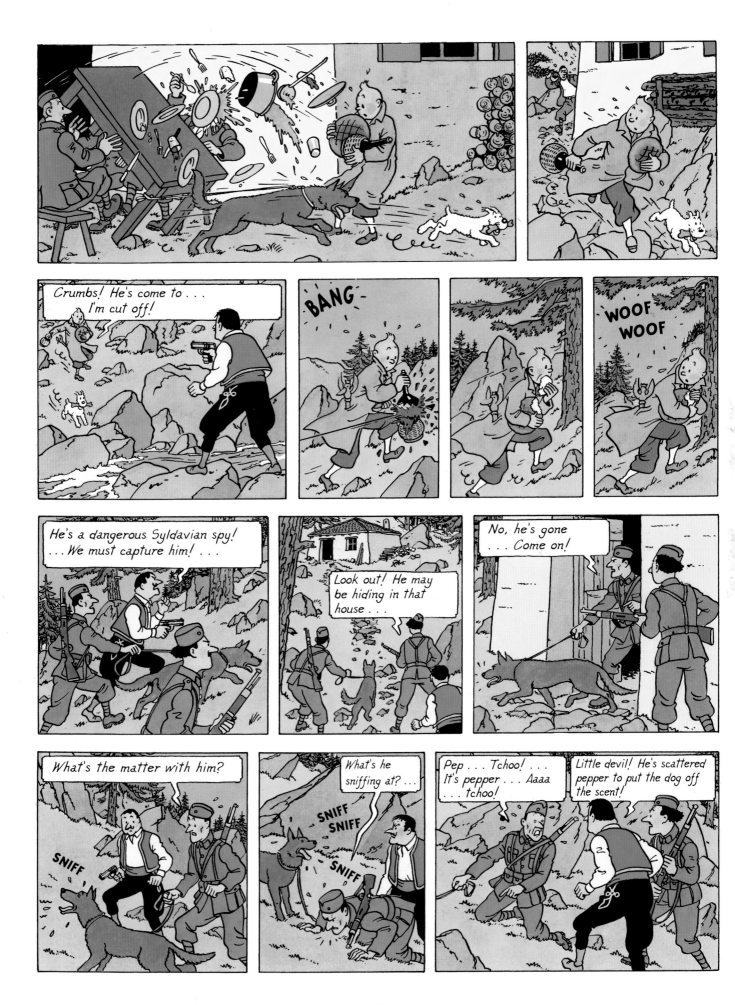

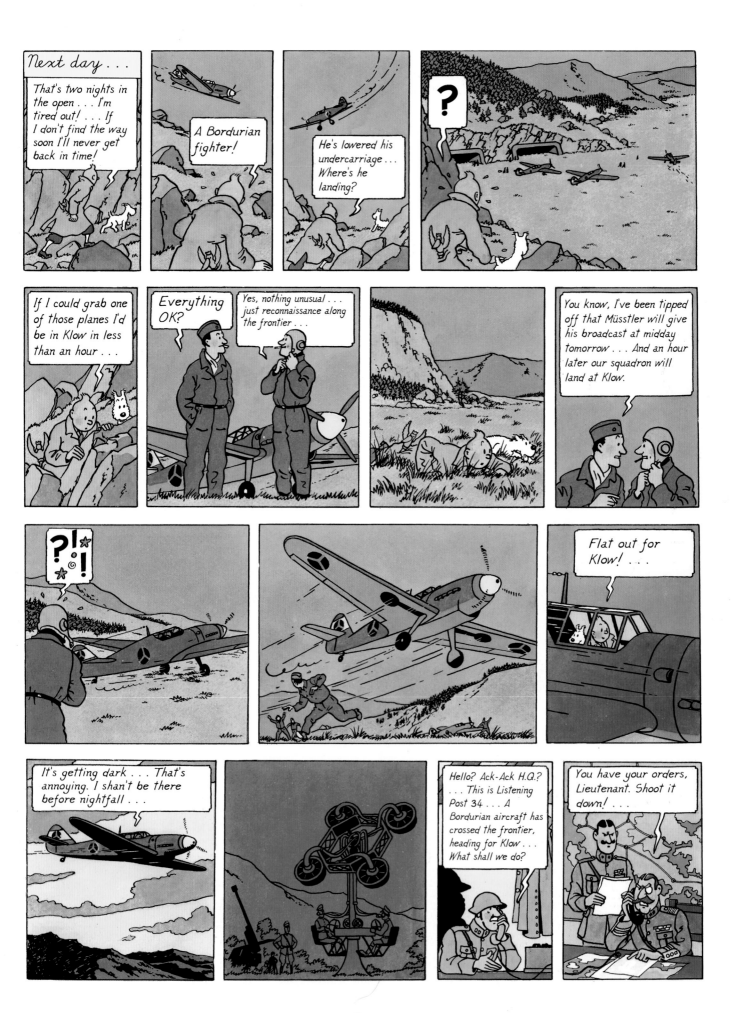

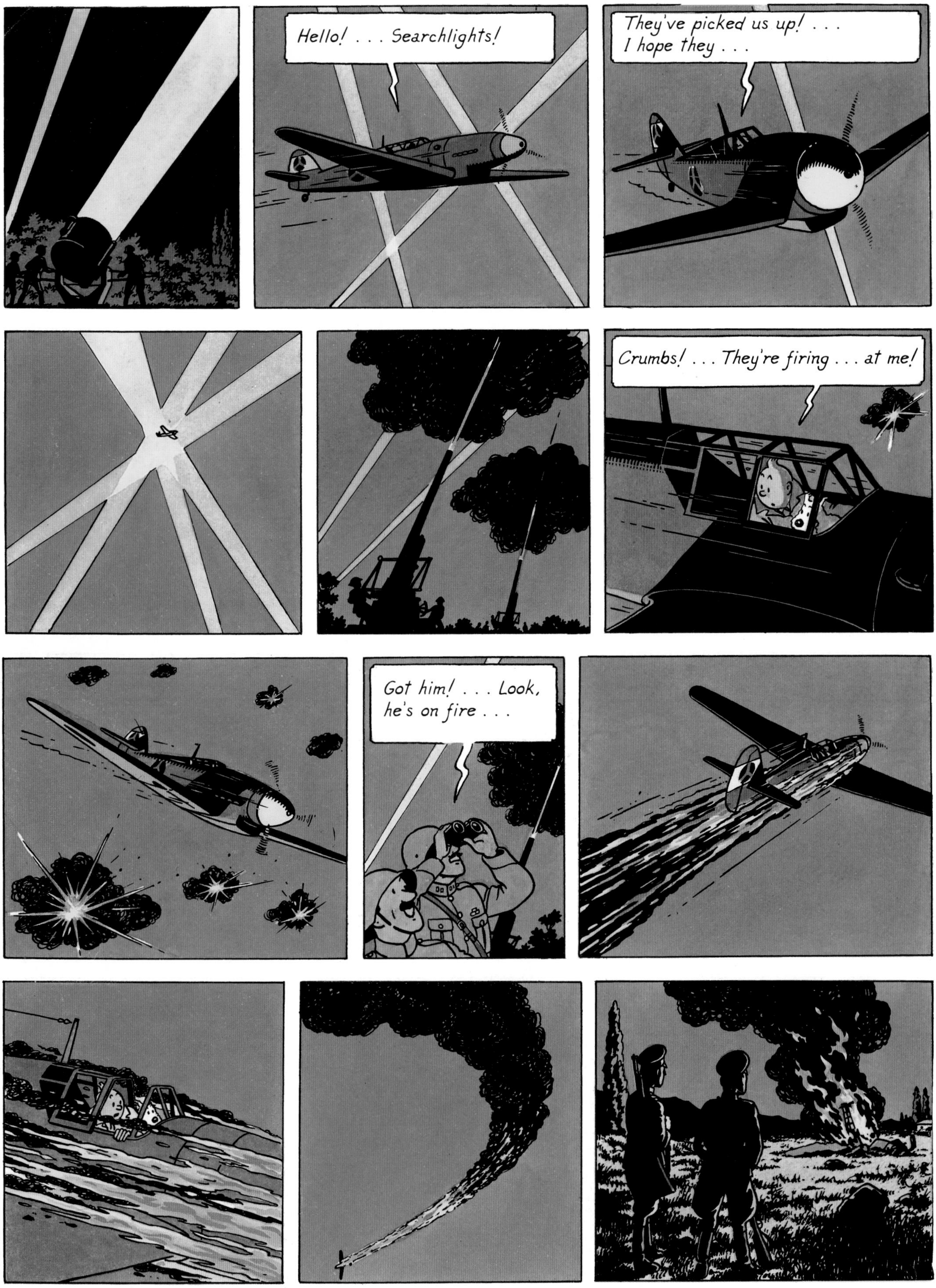
Hello! . . . Searchlights!
They've picked us up! . . . I hope they . . .
Crumbs! . . . They're firing . . . at me!
Got him! . . . Look, he's on fire . . .

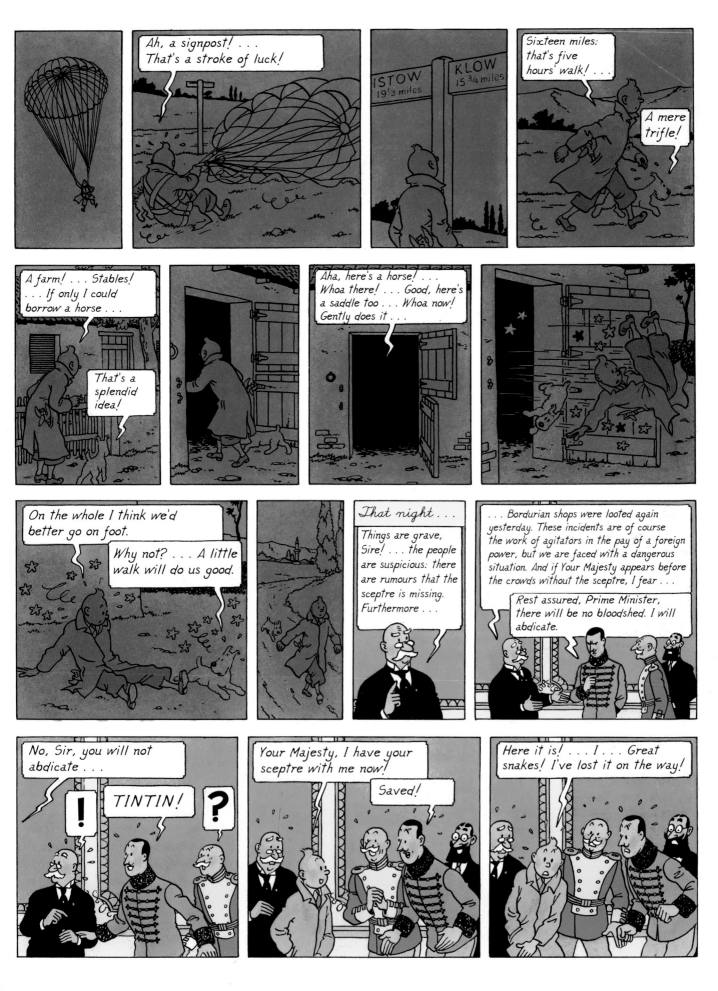

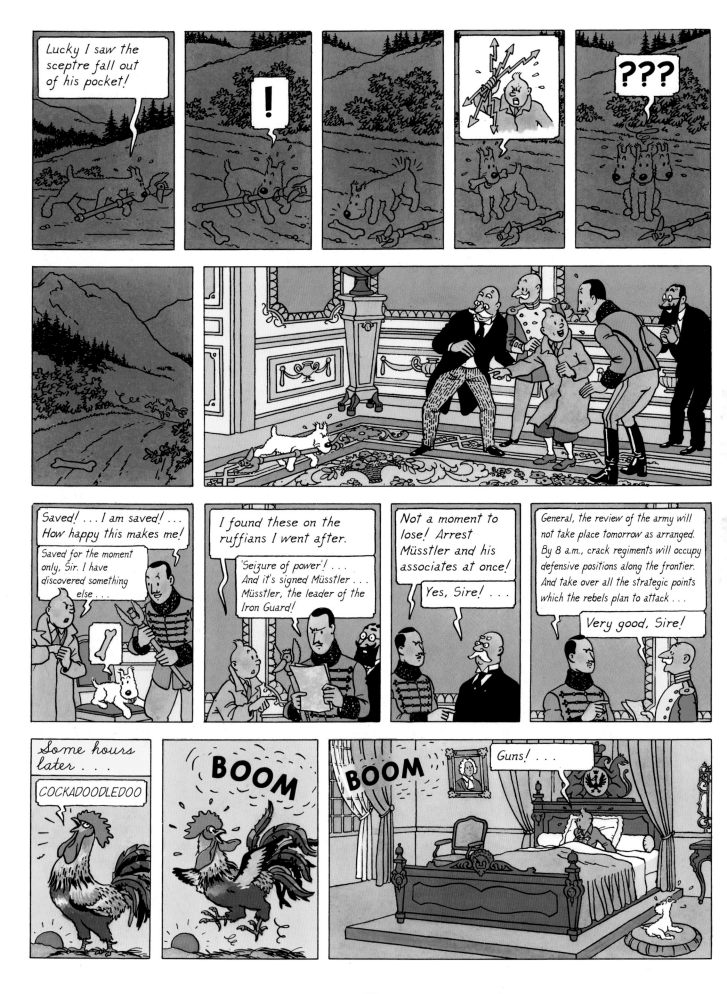

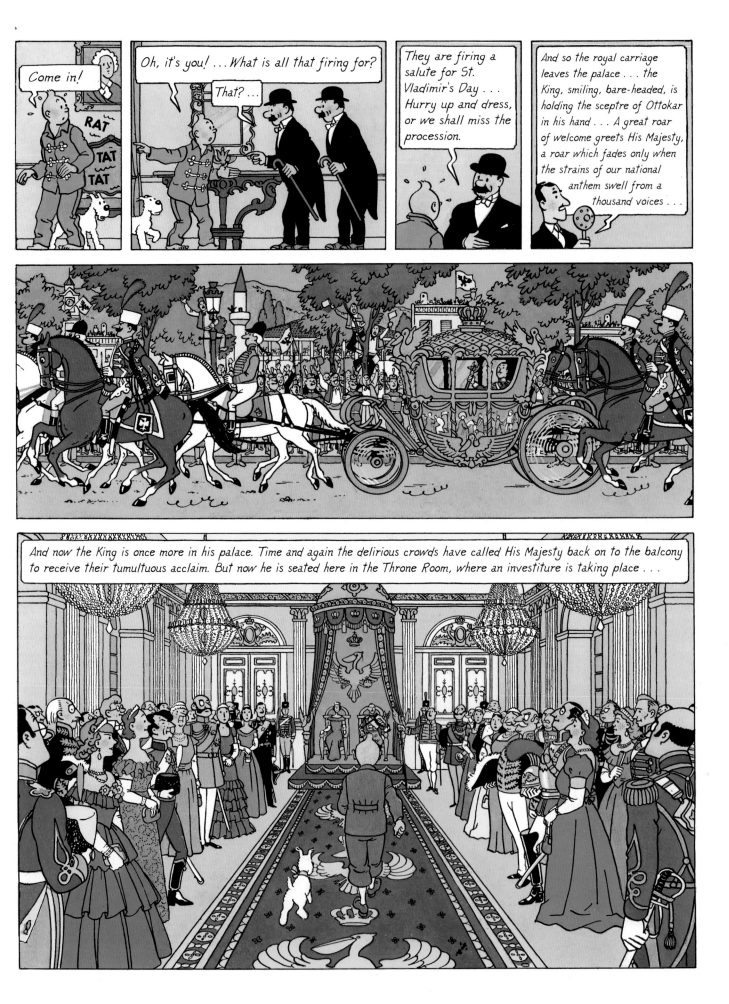

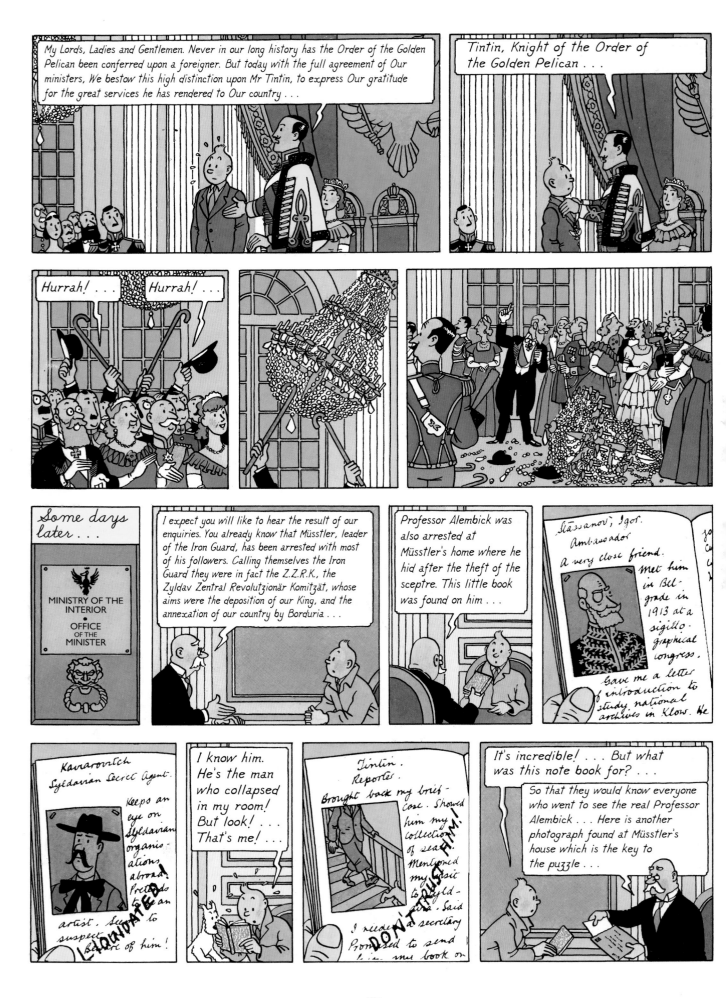

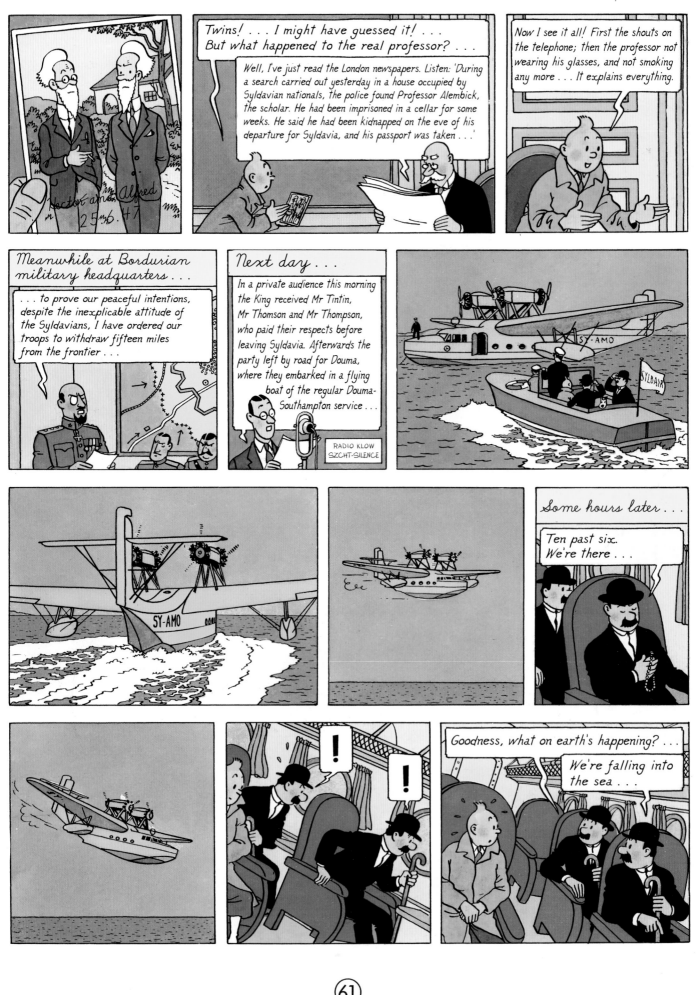

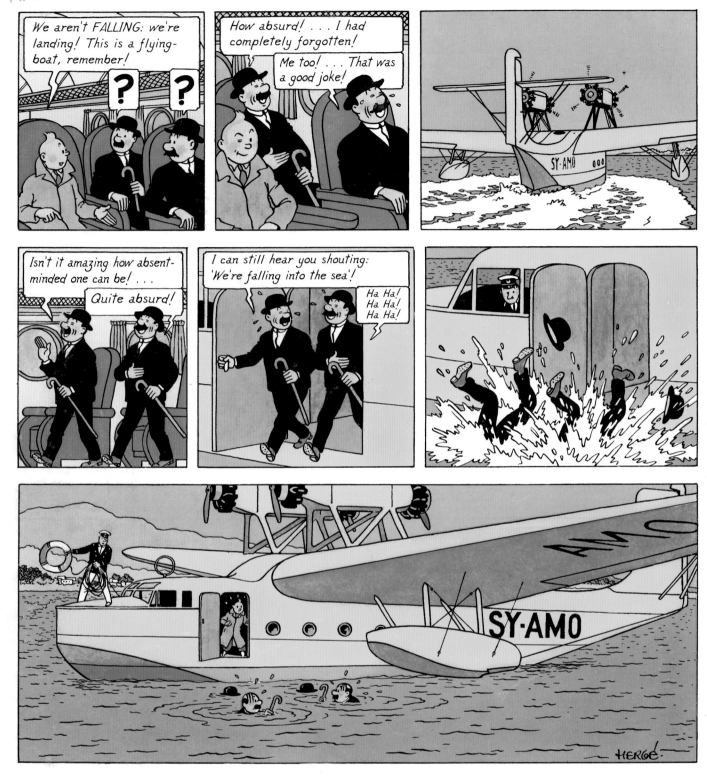

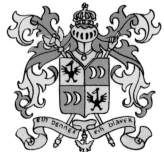

The TINTIN books are published in the following languages:

Alsacien	CASTERMAN
Basque	ELKAR
Bengali	ANANDA
Bernese	EMMENTALER DRUCK
Breton	AN HERE
Catalan	CASTERMAN
Chinese	CASTERMAN/CHINA CHILDREN PUBLISHING
Corsican	CASTERMAN
Danish	CARLSEN
Dutch	CASTERMAN
English	EGMONT UK LTD/LITTLE, BROWN & CO.
Esperanto	ESPERANTIX/CASTERMAN
Finnish	OTAVA
French	CASTERMAN
Gallo	RUE DES SCRIBES
Gaumais	CASTERMAN
German	CARLSEN
Greek	CASTERMAN
Hebrew	MIZRAHI
Indonesian	INDIRA
Italian	CASTERMAN
Japanese	FUKUINKAN
Korean	CASTERMAN/SOL
Latin	ELI/CASTERMAN
Luxembourgeois	IMPRIMERIE SAINT-PAUL
Norwegian	EGMONT
Picard	CASTERMAN
Polish	CASTERMAN/MOTOPOL
Portuguese	CASTERMAN
Provençal	CASTERMAN
Romanche	LIGIA ROMONTSCHA
Russian	CASTERMAN
Serbo-Croatian	DECJE NOVINE
Spanish	CASTERMAN
Swedish	CARLSEN
Thai	CASTERMAN
Tibetan	CASTERMAN
Turkish	YAPI KREDI YAYINLARI

TRANSLATED BY
LESLIE LONSDALE-COOPER AND MICHAEL TURNER

EGMONT
We bring stories to life

Artwork copyright © 1947 by Editions Casterman, Paris and Tournai.
Copyright © renewed 1975 by Casterman.
Text copyright © 1958 by Egmont UK Limited.
First published in Great Britain in 1958 by Methuen Children's Books.
This edition published in 2008 by Egmont UK Limited,
239 Kensington High Street, London W8 6SA.

Library of Congress Catalogue Card Numbers Afor 7895 and R 599746

ISBN 978 1 4052 0619 8

Printed in China
9 10 8

HERGÉ
★
THE ADVENTURES OF
TINTIN
★
KING OTTOKAR'S SCEPTRE

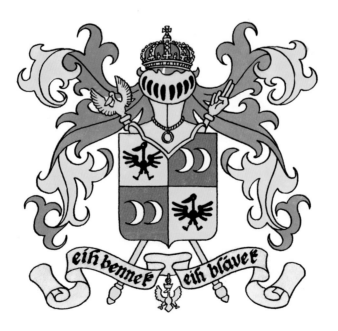

eih bennek eih blavek

EGMONT